TRULY U.

By

C. A. King

Happy Reading C.A.King

Cover Design:

Sarah Anderson Designs

Editor:

J.D. Cunegan

If you believe this book is dedicated to you,

perhaps it is!

Cover Design: **Sarah Anderson Designs**

First Printing: October 29, 2018

Re-prints: December 29, 2018; April 1, 2019

ISBN: 978-1-988301-62-4

Kings Toe Publishing

kingstoepublishing@gmail.com

Brantford, Ontario. Canada

Prologue

Her small toes wiggled in protest - warm feet had no business touching a cold wooden floor. Truly searched for her slippers, but they were missing. Without them, she'd be much louder walking about, but there was no choice. She was thirsty. Without a sip or two of water, she would never fall back to sleep.

Trying to take as few steps as possible, she crept in slow motion. The creaking groans of the wooden floor beneath her needed to be kept as silent as possible. That wasn't an easy task in her flannel nightgown. She had outgrown it at some point in the last year, but it hadn't yet been replaced and probably wouldn't be anytime soon.

The bathroom light hummed as it warmed up, adjusting the level of brightness as it did. She hopped up on a foot stool to reach for her cup, only to find it too was missing. Her head bent down to sip from the tap, but her long hair fell in the sink instead. Even tied back in a braid, it was always causing her problems. A sigh escaped slightly parted lips. The only way she was going to have a drink was if she ventured downstairs. She opted to sit at the top of them instead.

If she listened closely to the chattering below, an opportunity to sneak around her mother's party was sure to arise. There always came a point when everyone grew tired and fell asleep. That was the best part of every evening.

*****

"Full house!" Geena yelled, tossing her cards on the table. "Aces and kings." Her laughter rolled in waves as she pulled the pile of miscellaneous items into her stash.

The group was well past the use of money for the night. That ran out after the first two rounds. Geena twirled a pair of men's boxer shorts around in the air.

"If you plan on playing another round, you'll have to wager with your services." Tim laughed. "If I win, I'll trade him to you, Geena." He fired off a wink across the table.

"You aren't far behind me," Edgar scoffed. "These ladies are cheating!" His voice raised, but smile widened. His cards landed in the middle of the table face-down. The hand he'd been dealt wasn't worth showing. He ran his fingers over his stomach, playing with his own belly button in full view of anyone willing to watch.

"How about you get me a beer so I can see those buns?" Geena asked, chuckling at her man trying to be sexy. He didn't have a clue what that actually entailed. For her, making people enjoy her movements was a profession. Strippers relied on those talents for large tips.

"You laugh now, woman," Edgar said, "wait till after the company leaves and I'll be having my way with you." The sounds of small footsteps above them caught his attention. "Truly's up, wandering about again."

"Awe," Michelle cooed. "That's adorable. I don't know how you do it... raising a child and all. How old is she now?"

"She'll be turning nine real soon," Geena replied, twisting off the cap on a new bottle of beer. She gulped back a quarter of it before coming up for air.

"I didn't realize you two had been together that long," Michelle commented, exchanging glances between them. "Oh... sorry. I just assumed."

"No need to be sorry," Edgar said. "I love the kid to pieces. She might as well be my own."

"Geena," Michelle said, "I'm totally jealous. How'd you find such a great guy?"

"He was god sent, that's for sure," Geena smirked. "I was down on my luck and made some poor choices. When you have nothing and are hungry, you'll do anything for a meal and place to stay." Her eyes dulled. "I was no different."

"Oh my god, girl," Michelle blurted out. "I had no idea. What happened?"

Geena shrugged her shoulders, her bleach blond ponytail swaying behind them. "I met a crooked man. He wasn't much to look at... rather creepy... tall and thin. He offered me room and board if I serviced him. The minute we found out I was expecting, he tossed me out the door... said it wasn't in the cards. He was always big on checking his fortune before doing anything." She rolled her eyes. "I didn't believe in all that hocus pocus, but went along with it."

"No!" Michelle gasped.

"What we had was a business arrangement," Geena stated, "nothing more. I couldn't stand him. He smelt like the woods; that damp earthy smell after it rains." She shivered, goosebumps forming on her arms. "I was seventeen with a newborn baby and few options, especially with Truly's psycho dad out of the picture.

It was total abandonment. I never saw him again. That's when I became a dancer."

"I met her a few months later," Edgar added, putting his hand on hers. "Maybe it was in the stars." He chuckled. "My mom used to fool around with reading cards. She always said she could see the future."

"Did she use one of those fancy decks?" Tim asked, ribbing his friend.

"Naw," Edgar answered. "We didn't have money for that. She used an ordinary deck just like we are."

"If these hold the future," Geena joked, "why didn't you know you were going to lose all your clothes?" A single card flew through the air, landing face up directly in front of her boyfriend.

Edgar picked it up and twirled it around. "Ace of spades," he declared. "That there is the death card. You planning on knocking me off, woman?"

Geena laughed. "For what? You got an insurance policy I don't know about?"

"No, ma'am," Edgar replied. "It's much safer to be a broke bastard, if you ask me. That way there is nothing to collect if I am gone."

Geena leaned forward. Her lips grazed his. The phone buzzed, interrupting the moment. "Dang!" she exclaimed. "Charity is a no-show again tonight. Looks like I have to go to work."

"Hey," Edgar complained. "I never had a chance to win my clothes back and take a few off you ladies."

"You know we could use the extra money," Geena argued. "Besides, you can dream about me. In the morning, I'll make it all worthwhile."

"Promise?" Edgar smirked.

"Promise," Geena replied, waggling her eyebrows suggestively. His own boxers hit him in the face. "Put on some clothes until then." She glanced at the bottle in his hand. "Guess I'll take a cab."

"No need. We'll drop you," Tim offered. "I'm not willing to wait till morning." He grabbed Michelle's waist and pulled her in. "Hold on to your high heels, baby. You are in for one hell of a ride tonight. I feel like I could go for hours."

Edgar gulped back the last swallow of his beer, watching the trio leave. He glanced down. "And I get stuck all hot and bothered," he muttered, cracking his neck. He tossed aside the briefs, opting for track pants instead. One foot tangled going in, causing him to stumble. Frustration mutated into anger. His fists came down on the table, sending empty bottles toppling over. Only one remained standing.

"Waste not, want not," he huffed, grabbing Geena's still half-full beer and swooshing it back. Alcohol merely served to further fuel his rage.

When he let Geena and her kid move in, he anticipated her taking on a more physical role in his life. It sounded good in theory; a stripper at his beck and call, bending to his every distorted fantasy. Instead, he ended up with a woman who spent more time pleasing other men then she did him. What made it even worse, he seemed to always be the one left cleaning up the messes. He tossed a dish into the sink, not caring whether or not it broke.

His neck twisted from side to side, letting out another loud crack. His fists clenched tightly, to the point of his knuckles turning white. He was a volcano ready to explode. His heart pumped double time, red creeping into his face, gauging his rising body temperature like an old-fashioned thermometer. He glanced around, sizing up which wall was going to be the recipient of his mounting fury. Choosing one wasn't going to be easy. They all already had numerous spots poorly patched from previous outbursts.

Glancing up at the ceiling, a grin, more crooked than a used-car salesman, crept over his face. His tongue darted out, wetting partly open lips.

Grabbing his belt off the table, he headed to the stairs, taking each one as a predator stalking prey. A pitter-patter of scurrying feet deepened the lines of the sinister smile on his face. His pace quickened. He snapped the belt between his hands.

The silver door handle felt cold against his skin. It turned easily in his grip; it always did. He peeked in at a bundle of shaking blankets in the middle of a single mattress.

"Truly," Edgar called out. "You've been a bad girl. You left your slippers and cup lying around. You know there are rules in my house. I'm going to have to punish you. I've already thrown them out. You need to learn to behave." He closed the door behind him.

Chapter One

Fifteen years later.

Her hands smoothed over her short black hair. Sucking in her gut, Truly held up a fist, poised to knock. Releasing the air she was holding, she shook her head at her own ridiculous attitude. There was no need to be as nervous as she had been going to her first appointment. She licked her lips, nodding. Her knuckles landed firm against the wooden door.

"Come in," Doctor Stevenson called out, expecting her. "Please have a seat."

"Thank you," Truly replied, almost losing her balance on the gleaming imported tile.

Clumsiness joined her almost everywhere she went, but in her doctor's office, her lack of coordination heightened tenfold. It was more of a signature move, happening every time she visited. Why the man kept the floors polished to the point of being slippery was beyond her. She settled on it being an odd test of some sort - one she never seemed to be able to pass. Did being clumsy affect one's mental health? It didn't seem likely for there to be a correlation between the two, but then she wasn't the psychiatrist.

"Tell me how things have been," the doctor ordered. "Is there anything specific you want to discuss this week before we get started?"

"I'm still having trouble sleeping. The nightmares have been bothering me," she answered. "I wake up drenched in my own sweat, but can't recall anything from the dream. After that, I toss and turn until morning."

"Yes," the doctor replied. "Until we are able to regain your lost memories, I'm afraid the dreams will continue. It's your subconscious trying to break through the barrier. If I prescribe a sleep aid, it might interfere with our progress. I'd prefer not to do that."

"But I've been at this for years and I still can't remember a single detail from my childhood," she complained. "Nothing is working."

"The mind is a delicate thing," the doctor stated. "It compensates in inexplicable ways for situations it believes a person cannot handle. In some instances, individuals end up living out fantasies in their own minds; in others, multiple personalities are established. In cases such as your own, it blocks hurtful memories. I have no doubt there are many dark things in your past... things you need to come to terms with. This process cannot be rushed. If you stop now, you might never regain the memories you lost. Is that what you want?"

"I'm working three jobs just to be here," Truly scoffed. "What do you think?" Her shoulders shrugged, allowing her hands to fall into her lap, neatly folding together over faded blue jeans.

"Shall we continue, then?" the doctor suggested. "I don't want to waste any more of your hard-earned money."

Truly nodded.

"Good," the doctor said, fiddling with a stack of white cards on his desk. "I'd like to try some suggestive imagery."

Truly sighed. "Ink spots again?" she complained. "Haven't I done this enough times before?" They were her least favourite of the exercises psychiatrists had picked for her over the years. Pretending to envision something that wasn't there never made sense to her. In the end, the only thing she ever saw was spilled black paint.

"Humour me," Doctor Stevenson ordered. "Tell me what you see and don't leave out anything." He held up the first card, watching her facial expressions.

"A frightened squid," Truly blurted out.

The doctor frowned, placing the card face down to his left, forming the beginnings of a second pile. Other than a steno notebook and an office telephone, the cards were the only things on the old-fashioned oak desk. He flashed a second card, hoping for a better result.

"A frightened octopus," Truly said, her face remaining emotionless.

"You already used that one," the doctor complained. "I need you to be serious."

"A squid and an octopus are two very different creatures," Truly argued. "I can see them quite clearly... can't you?" The onset of a grin sprouted at the corners of her mouth.

"And this one," the doctor asked, disappointment already flickering in his hazel eyes. His unscripted flashes of emotion sparked her curiosity.

In his prime, Doctor Stevenson probably hadn't been hard on the eyes. His hair, now thinning, still for the most part, held onto its original dark brown shade, although strands of white were making appearances. Unlike some men his age, he hadn't given up on his physique. His well-tailored suit, handcrafted to fit his form, wasn't designed to hide any extra pounds.

Rather than studying her next black hole, Truly found herself wondering why her doctor was single. She had come to that conclusion based solely on the overwhelming lack of anything around him proving the existence of a family. There was no ring on his finger or photographs on his desk. In fact, there were no personal items at all in his office.

Of course, she hadn't actually asked him to confirm her suspicions. Most men would take that as a blatant attempt on her part to flirt. Truth be told, she wasn't interested in men or women in a romantic way. Perhaps he was similar to her when it came to romance.

The same flicker that had stolen away her thoughts dragged her back to the task at hand. There was no need to anger the only person trying to help her, even if she was paying him.

Truly glanced at the splotch, knowing she wasn't getting away with another snarky response. Her lips pursed together, jutting out slightly. "Grass," she answered.

"Grass?"

"Yes," Truly replied. "A meadow of long grass. I think it's growing."

"Good," the doctor said with a satisfied nod. "Now we are getting somewhere. And this one?"

Truly shifted her position. The seat itself wasn't the problem. It had been designed to provide the utmost comfort in an elegant style and could even recline, if that was what she wanted. The picture was what made her uncomfortable. That and her inability to look away from it.

"Truly?" the doctor said, questioning her silence.

"I... um," she stuttered. "It's a chair... no, it is more of a throne, sitting on a black and white checkerboard-style floor. Trees line the edges of the tiles for as far as I can see. Perfectly formed petals are floating down from the sky."

The doctor's brows arched. He turned the card to examine the ink spot, breaking his patient's trance. "Are you playing games?" he questioned. "Did you really see all that?"

"I did," Truly admitted. "It was as clear as a painting. I can still visualize it in my mind."

"And this one?" He held up another card.

"It looks like someone ran over a bunny," Truly snickered. "That's roadkill."

"Well," Doctor Stevenson said, placing his glasses still open on the pile containing finished cards, while he rubbed his eyes. "I think we have made a small breakthrough today."

"What now?" Truly asked. "Shock treatments?" She snorted at her own joke.

"I want you to take this picture with you," he answered in a stern voice. "When you come across any instances of deja vu, check if your vision from today has any more to show. Use your surroundings in a similar manner."

"What do you mean?" Truly questioned, her brow wrinkling. "What surroundings?"

"Look at the clouds or in pools of water," he explained. "Use them in an identical fashion as we did here today with the ink spots. Try to tune in to what your subconscious is trying to tell you. That's the whole point here... your conscious and subconscious need to meet in the middle and acknowledge one another again."

"And if something comes to me?" Truly asked.

"My door is always open," the doctor replied. "In the meantime, I'm switching up your medication. I'd like to, one day, ween you off drugs altogether. They might be adding to your mental block. I don't believe you are psychotic."

"Is that safe?" Truly asked. "I was told I needed to remain on them for life."

"I'm not, at the moment, taking you off medication completely," the doctor answered, smiling. "I'm just taking you down a notch or two. I am setting up an appointment with a colleague who specializes in hypnosis, as well. I am asking him to attempt to safely reach your younger self that way. If we can find out what happened in your past that frightened you into memory loss, we can begin to repair the damage."

"You'll be in touch, then?" Truly questioned.

"My secretary will call you when we have all the details," he replied, pulling out a white pad of paper and a pen from his top drawer. He scribbled a few lines before ripping the top page off. "Here you are. Start these immediately and discontinue the others. If you don't hear from me sooner, I'll see you next week."

"Thank you," Truly said, accepting the prescription. A frown crossed her face on the way out. She could never read the man's writing. That meant she'd have to wait for the bus ride home from the pharmacy to check out her new pills online.

Chapter Two

The bus rolled to stop beside the town centre. Truly glanced around, knowing most of the other passengers were headed to the same area as her. However, they were content to continue riding for another half an hour rather than taking the short walk through the park. Even in smaller towns, hustle and bustle had replaced stopping to smell the roses.

"Thanks, Stan," Truly said, hopping down the steps to the sidewalk. He was the regular driver for almost every route she needed to take and, in ways, had become her confidant. She didn't have a lot of friends and even if she had there wasn't much time in her schedule to squeeze them in. Being friendly with Stan allowed her to multitask. He drove while they talked. There was no pressure on her to watch her words, either. Stan was happily married and a proud father.

"See you tomorrow," he replied before closing the doors and continuing on.

Knollville wasn't a big city, but it wasn't a hick town either. The parks all showed evidence of that. A lot of taxpayer funds went into maintaining the well-sculpted gardens and ornamental trees. A team of construction workers blocking off a section of pavement for repairs was proof in the making. Soon, the cracks everyone tried so hard not to step on were sure to be smoothed over with a fresh layer of concrete. There were women willing to pay a fortune to have a similar procedure done to the lines on their faces.

As she approached the middle of the park, trickling water caught her attention, enticing her to watch it cascading down four tiers of basins before being recycled back to the top by a hidden pump, starting the entire process over again. Truly took a seat on the rim. Her fingers skimmed the top of the water, sending ripples across the surface and chills down her spine. The precious wishes of Knollville's residents reflected in the sun - as glorious as a pirate's treasure of pure silver and gold. This lot of coins, however, was slated to be plundered all too soon and probably used to pay for the repair crew lurking nearby, lunches in hand.

"Look for a vision," she mumbled, frowning. Her gaze locked onto her own reflection, searching for something to tell her who she was and what monsters lay in her past. She chuckled. "Guess I am the monster." She winked at her own image, receiving the same back in return.

A child's scream caught her attention, drawing her towards a commotion. She passed a group of parents chatting amongst themselves and oblivious to the playground drama unfolding beneath their noses. Even a baby's cries went unanswered. After several glares from dog walkers, the mother shook her head, pushing a soother into the child's mouth. A temporary fix meant to steal her a few more precious minutes of socializing before she was forced to return to a life where the only words her companion spoke were mama and dada, the latter being the preference.

Truly took a seat on one of the empty benches scattered around the area. She pulled out a plastic bag of crackers. A group of pigeons gathered at her feet, anticipating a few crumbs being dropped their way. They weren't disappointed. After nibbling at a corner, she broke one into several pieces, tossing them in as many directions as she could. It never made a difference. The largest birds always won out.

"You have to be faster," she said to the runt. Another piece landed in front of the smallest of her new feathered friends. She shook her head, watching a larger pigeon plow over the smaller one, stealing the scrap.

Bullies always were found in playgrounds.

"You aren't allowed to play with us!" A blonde girl screamed. "This club is for kids who have fathers." Using the palms of both of her hands, she pushed a second girl to the ground, laughing. The other children were quick to join in.

The frown lines on Truly's face deepened. Her eyes stung, tears threatening to fall. It took all of her self-control to refrain from running to the aid of the young victim. That wasn't her place, though. Instead, she was forced to watch from the sidelines as the onslaught of insults continued until the girl finally broke. Tears were exactly what a bully wanted.

She wasn't sure why she felt such a deep connection to the youngster still sitting on her backside in the sand, but she did. She also knew any adult advice the child received would have been flawed.

Don't let it bother you, or *don't cry, you are just empowering them,* sounded good in a speech. In reality, the youngster would only end up suffering longer following those suggestions. Getting it over with was a better course of action. At least then, the verbal abuse would stop. Giving in was the only way to make it end. No one was coming to help. In real life, there were no superheros to swoop in and save the day, especially for a child without a father.

She glanced up at the clouds, looking for a pattern. The fluffy white pillows floated carefree, begging her to join them...

*****

"Why are you alone?" Jeffrey asked.

"Because," Priscilla said, her hands crossed behind her back, "she doesn't have a father. You can't bring to school what you don't have."

"I do so!" Truly yelled back.

"Nah-uh," Priscilla argued, playing with a blue ribbon tied to one of her blonde braids. "My mom says he is only pretending to be your father. He isn't even married to your mom. Besides, if he was your dad, he'd be here, wouldn't he? I don't see him. Mom says he doesn't even have a job. That means he didn't have anything else important to do and still couldn't be bothered to show up. That's not a father!"

"Priscilla," an elderly gentleman in a three-piece suit called out. "Come show me your work, sweetheart."

"Coming, Father," Priscilla purred, skipping away. Her dress swished around her knees with every step.

"Don't listen to her," Jeffrey suggested once Priscilla was out of ear range. "I'm sure he was just busy."

"What does a father do?" Truly asked.

"What do you mean?" Jeffrey cocked his head, looking for his own answer.

"I mean," Truly replied, "what makes a person a father? How would I know if I had one?"

"I guess they are supposed to do things with their kids. You know... teach us stuff," Jeffrey said. "Mine showed me how to fish last weekend. I caught one this big." He outstretched his arms as far as they would reach. "That was my first time in a boat, too."

"Is that it?" Truly questioned, a pout attaching itself to her lips. "Just teach us stuff?"

"I don't know," Jeffrey admitted. "I think they are supposed to help take care of us... keep us safe and stuff and prepare us for the future. They also give their kids gifts. Mine brings me home something from every trip he takes."

"Edgar doesn't really do any of that," Truly muttered. "Maybe Priscilla is right, maybe I don't have a dad... not a real one, anyway."

*****

Two dogs exchanging greetings in the distance brought her back to reality. Truly rubbed the back of her neck, a stiffness having set in from her recent bout of cloud gazing. She glanced around at the stillness that had replaced the bustling activity from earlier. Even the workers had vacated. Goosebumps formed on her arms. How long had she been daydreaming? She rubbed both hands over her face as other questions filled her head. Was that a memory or had she made it up after seeing the children arguing earlier?

She glanced at her watch, eyes widening. It was late. She'd have to run all the way to work to make it on time. The new prescription would have to wait another day. The doctor hadn't seemed concerned about her taking medicine. How much could it hurt if she was off it altogether for one day?

Chapter Three

"Damn," Truly said, slamming the fridge door.

"Broken?"

Truly jumped. "Oi! What are you doing in here?" she asked. "It is polite to knock before entering, you know."

"I think your lock's broken," Maria answered. "The door pushed open when I tried to knock." She pulled herself into a sitting position on the kitchen counter, dangling feet banging against the bottom cupboards.

"Great," Truly replied, rolling her eyes. "I can add that to the growing list of things that need to be repaired."

"Fridge?"

"Yeah," Truly answered. "It must have shut off yesterday sometime. It's already warm inside. Dry cereal?"

Maria took the box. Her hand plunged in, wiggling around a bit before emerging stuffed full of mini dried marshmallows.

"How do you do that?" Truly asked. "I don't know anyone who can feel their way around the actual cereal parts."

Maria laughed. "I grew up with five brothers. If I wanted any chance at the sugar, I had to be quick. It's amazing what we can learn to do when pushed up against a wall."

"I wouldn't call missing out on sweets being pushed up against a wall," Truly said.

"Maybe not," Maria admitted, tossing a yellow star in the air and catching it in her mouth. "Your landlord has you up against one, though. When are you going to grow a set and tell this guy where to go? He needs to fix this place for you."

"Brilliant plan," Truly said, grabbing the box to fetch her own handful. She chuckled. Not one marshmallow surfaced. That summed up her life perfectly. "Then he can kick me out. I can't afford to move. No one in this building can. He knows it, too."

"There are laws," Maria argued, brushing her hands against each other to remove the remnants of cereal.

"The law doesn't always protect the innocent," Truly replied. "I can't take the chance. Besides, one day, his family will take over. I've heard they are much nicer to deal with."

"Maybe this will change your mind," Maria said, holding up and envelope. "It was taped to your door."

"You could have given it to me when you first came in," Truly complained, snatching the letter from her friend's hand.

"What fun would that be?" Maria shrugged her shoulders, her brows arching and falling along with them.

"It's from my landlord," Truly said, glaring at the logo imprinted in the left hand corner of the envelope. "I wonder what it is."

"You could open it and find out," Maria suggested. "That's what I'd do."

"Very funny," Truly snapped. "I can't handle any more bad news." She held the letter out, her eyes clenched closed. "You do it."

"Great," Maria said, grabbing the envelope back. "I should have just opened it before I came in."

"That would have been an invasion of my privacy," Truly declared.

"You are making me do it anyways," Maria argued, rolling her eyes. "What's the difference?"

"The difference is you have my permission to open it now," Truly replied. "What does it say?"

Maria stuck one of her long fingernails in the corner, using it as a letter opener. The paper inside made a crinkling noise as it opened.

"It says," Maria started, "Dear Ms Alaney... that would be you." She smiled. "We are lowering your rent by two hundred dollars a month."

"Really?!" Truly exclaimed.

"No," Maria admitted. "They are raising your rent by a hundred a month. If you want to dispute, you can contact Bernard Bailey directly... sorry." She hopped down, dropping the letter on the counter. "A bunch of us are going out tonight if you want to come along. It might do you good."

"I can't," Truly replied, picking up the letter. "I have to work at the restaurant."

"You work too much," Maria said. "You could use a night out once in a while. We are going to check out a new psychic shop that opened downtown. They do readings and everything. I want to know my future!"

"I hate fortunes. Besides, it will be a long while before I can go anywhere," Truly muttered. "I barely make ends meet as it is working three jobs. I have no idea where I am going to come up with another hundred dollars a month."

"You need to talk to him." Maria suggested. "He won't find a more perfect tenant. That counts for more than you think."

"You don't know Bernard," Truly scoffed.

Chapter Four

Truly pulled the door closed behind her. Rebelling against her will, it popped back open. The extent of the damage to the lock was far worse than she originally thought. One foot came down hard on the hallway's rust coloured carpeting before lashing out at the door frame. She bit her lip. The kick hurt her foot more than the building.

"Is everything okay?" Mrs. Evermore asked, peeking out of her apartment. "I heard some banging."

Truly threw her arms up in the air. Forcing a smile to form, she turned around to greet her neighbour.

The couple living in the apartment across from her own had been there since well before she moved in. In the past few years, she'd watch them transition from aging to elderly, growing grey gracefully before her eyes. Now they were the definition of what sweet grandparents should be - at least the stereotype. She couldn't remember if she ever met her own.

"Everything is fine," she lied. "I'm just having a bit of an argument with my door. It seems to be broken."

"Like everything else in this place," Mr. Evermore said, squeezing by his wife, toolbox in hand. "Let me take a look. Well, there's your problem. You need a new door handle." He scratched his back with his screwdriver. "I don't suppose you have an extra one lying around..." His eyebrows arched in anticipation of the answer.

"I'm afraid not," Truly said. "I never thought I'd need one. I never thought I'd need a lot of things when I took this apartment." The fridge was the worst of them all. No one kept a spare one of those lying around.

"One should always be prepared for the unexpected. I happen to have a door handle, but it's not meant for an entrance way. I grabbed it for our bathroom." He rummaged through his box. "Here it is. I'll put this one on for you. It's a quick fix until you can pick up a decent one."

"Thank you," Truly said, flashing a smile, the first real one in weeks. "Hopefully they have door handles at the store."

"I see you received the friendly note from our landlord," he mentioned. "It's bad enough he doesn't fix anything, now he's raising the rent, too."

"Are you thinking about fighting it?" Truly questioned.

"No," Mr. Evermore answered. "He knows we can't. Even if every tenant in the building joined forces, I don't think between the lot of us we'd come up with two nickels to rub together, let alone a retainer for legal representation."

"I don't know what we are going to do," Mrs. Evermore blurted out. "We are on a fixed income." Her hand stroked the fur of a ginger cat in her arms. "That man will reap what he sows one day. Mark my words. Karma doesn't take names."

"Here's the keys," Mr. Evermore said. The set jingled, dropping into her hand. "Let me know if you need any help installing the new one once you get it." His bones creaked as he bent down to gather his tools in a fashion almost as loud as his apartment door closing.

Truly glanced at her watch several times during the elevator ride down. When the double doors finally parted, they revealed a clear path leading outside. Instead of moving, she allowed the doors to close, taking away the option of escape.

She inhaled deeply, an exercise she'd been told helped calm nerves. It had never worked for her before and this time was no different. Extending a shaky finger, she pressed the button labelled *office*. The choice had been made. Still, there was an additional mustering of courage needed to follow through with her plan. It all started off with a simple stroll down the hallway to Bernard Bailey's combination office and apartment.

Truly found herself standing face-to-face with yet another door. Her heart skipped a beat and not in a good way. This nervousness was for a different reason. Bernard Bailey was one of the most unscrupulous men she'd ever encountered, and she'd met quite a few scumbags in her time.

Her knuckles whitened, waiting for their moment to shine. Biting her bottom lip, she allowed them to come in contact with the wood that stood between her and destiny. Her landlord, however, was the one to answer.

"Well," he said, his tongue swirling a toothpick around in his mouth. "What do we have here?"

Bernard Bailey was everything she despised - the worst of the worst when it came to men. He cared about nothing. Even his own family visited him as infrequently as possible.

"Mr. Bailey," Truly said, taking a step back to put some distance between herself and the stench of body odour that always accompanied the man.

As if sensing her thoughts, he lifted one arm, resting his hand on the door frame above. Fumes wafted down from the yellow stained pits of his undershirt. He chuckled at her apprehension.

"I wanted to discuss the rent increase," she explained, "and there are some things that need fixing in my apartment."

"Really?" Bernard scoffed, scratching his sagging belly with his free hand. It was allowed to flop freely, his pants being fastened under the bulge, rather than around his waist. The undershirt was too small to effectively conceal it. "What sort of things?"

"My door, for one." Truly bit her lip, attempting to stop it from quivering. "My fridge doesn't seem to be working, either, and I'm still waiting for the oven to be replaced."

"I see," Bernard replied, his oversized nostrils flaring. "And you expect me to do what?"

"Fix things!" Truly exclaimed. She paused, seeing the man hadn't flinched a muscle. "And the increase in rent is preposterous. I already work three jobs to afford living here as it is."

"If you can't afford to pay it, that is a problem," he replied, pulling the toothpick from his mouth. He sucked air through a gap in his teeth, creating a low-pitched whistle. "I like you. I'm going to make a proposal. You seem like a hard worker... eager to please your bosses. I'm going to offer you a job."

"A job?" Truly echoed.

"Yes," Bernard replied. "You satisfy me and I'll knock off the extra rent and then some. If you go out of your way to do a little extra to please me, I'll even make sure everything is fixed. Sound good?"

"It does," Truly admitted. "What would I be doing? Cleaning? Paperwork?"

"Oh, no." Bernard chuckled. "Nothing that strenuous. You'll be doing all your work on your back." He laughed. "I suppose occasionally on your knees... or all fours."

Truly gasped. "You can't be serious. Sex isn't a job!"

"I beg to differ," Bernard argued. "It's the oldest profession in the book. It's also the only way I am willing to offer your pretty ass a break." He stepped aside, using his eyes to suggest she enter.

Truly glanced at her watch. "I'm late for work," she squeaked, backing up. Her stride quickened to a jog then an all-out run.

"When you are ready," Bernard yelled after her, "I'll be here waiting."

Chapter Five

One of the things she always liked best about working as a cashier in a *we sell just about everything* store was how fast the time passed. Under her current circumstances, however, that evening's shift went a little too quick for her liking. Home wasn't where she wanted to be. Between the door lock and Bernard, it definitely wasn't a place she felt safe. She glanced at her plastic bag. At least the handle could be fixed.

She sighed, stopping at the elevator only long enough to read the note taped over the buttons: *Use Stares*. She shook her head. Bernard Bailey was a real piece of work. She hadn't made it further than the end of high school, but at least she could spell.

There were a lot of places where Truly enjoyed taking the stairs. Her building was not one of them. She inhaled deeply before heading up the first flight. It was a pointless gesture. At some point before her floor, she'd be forced to breathe in the strong chemical odour that accompanied the trip. Most of the other tenants weren't about to complain about the stench. To them, it meant the landlord was at least trying to keep the bug population under control. The hint of lemon that accompanied the bug spray smell threw up warning signs for Truly. In her opinion, Bernard merely sprayed a can of household pest killer in the common areas himself. That would do little against infestations.

The sigh of relief that accompanied making it to her floor quickly turned into a gasp of horror. Her door was open... again. This time, however, Bernard and some men were inside, poking about.

"What are you doing?" Truly asked.

"Removing the fridge and stove," Bernard answered. "You did say they were broken."

"Yes," Truly admitted. "I never agreed..."

Bernard held up one hand. "I'm taking them out on my own," he stated, interrupting her. "No need to thank me. I'll even see to the disposal."

Truly glanced at her old fridge passing by on its way out, then around her apartment. Her eyes settled on her slightly ajar bedroom door. It had been closed when she left for work. She shivered at the thought of Bernard Bailey going through her personal items. The taste of bile began to rise in her throat. She gulped it back down.

"When can I expect the new ones?" Truly questioned.

Her landlord chuckled. "New ones? Who said anything about new ones? I certainly didn't."

The men removing her stove chuckled as they exited the room. "Which apartment next, boss?"

"Take five," Bernard offered. "I'll be down in a minute to pick up the rest of the paperwork."

"I don't understand," Truly started.

"Don't understand what?" Bernard snickered. "After our little chat today, I made an executive decision. From now on, appliances are not included in the rent of any of my units. It is up to the tenant to supply their own." He winked.

"You can't do that!" Truly shrieked.

"I can," he said, pushing a piece of paper into her chest, making sure to allow his hand to brush dangerously close to her breast at the same time. "And I did. The paperwork is legit and legal. Oh. Here's the bill for the locksmith work."

"You broke the door!" Truly complained. "Why do I have to pay for it?"

"Check your lease," Bernard answered. "In subsection fifty-four, it states quite clearly that all tenants... that's you, shall provide the landlord... that's me, with a copy of the key to the exterior door of their unit."

"I had to go to work," Truly complained.

"You were at my office," Bernard argued. "That gave you enough opportunity to offer a set to me. You chose not to. This is what happens if you don't follow the terms of your rental agreement. I'll expect payment within two weeks."

Truly grabbed the new handle from inside the plastic bag she was carrying. Ripping into the packaging, she removed the soon-to-be keys. "Here! Now you have a copy."

"You seem a bit stressed," Bernard snickered. "There is a solution to all that bothers you." A lopsided grin accompanied his words. "I'm available day or night."

She threw the packaging at the door as it closed behind him, sinking to floor in tears.

"How on earth am I getting through this?" she mumbled.

You know how.

"Who said that?!" Truly yelled, jumping to her feet. "Who's here?"

No one answered.

Truly grabbed a knife from her kitchen drawer, wincing at the open space where appliances should have been. Each step was placed with purpose as she crept to the bathroom and flung open the door. Using the blade edged side of the knife, she opened the floral shower curtain, exposing only the aging tub.

She allowed herself to breathe again before heading to check out the final room; her bedroom. The door creaked open slowly. Her hand felt the inside wall, flicking on the lights. The closet was her first search mission; after fighting with and becoming entangled in her own sweaters, she moved on to check under the bed.

Nothing! she thought, taking a seat. An open drawer caught her attention. Her hand covered her mouth. Several pairs of underwear were missing.

Nausea overtook her. There was no stopping the vomit. She raced for the toilet, barely making it to the white bowl before losing all she had eaten for the day. She watched it swirl away before feeling strong enough to brush her teeth. She kept her focus on the running water, not wanting to gaze into her own eyes for fear of what she might see.

You are not your mother.

Truly sniffled, laughing at the same time. "Great, I'm literally going crazy. This warrants a trip to the good doctor."

He can't help you like I can. You know what to do. Help them see their future and I'll take care of the rest.

Truly swallowed back a mouthful of over-the-counter liquid sleep aid straight from the bottle. Flopping back on the bed, she stared at the ceiling, begging for the sandman to take her quickly. In the morning she could figure out how to deal with hearing voices. The woodsy scent of forests floated past her nostrils, carrying her away to a better place than she was in. There would be no nightmares that evening. Her real life had enough of those.

Chapter Six

Truly opened her eyes and glanced around the room. Her open underwear draw was indication enough that it hadn't all been a nightmare. Pulling herself into a sitting position, she reached for her phone.

"No. No. No. No. No!" she shrieked. "I paid you. I know I did. Please don't be dead."

All the pleading in the world wasn't going to make a dial tone suddenly appear. She tossed her phone on the mattress.

"Another beautiful day in hell," she huffed, heading to the kitchen. "At least the coffee maker still works." She flicked the switch before grabbing her purse.

Pulling a box of crackers out of an otherwise bare cupboard, she refilled her plastic bag and returned it. The black-ink stained card caught her attention. Coffee mug in hand, she focused on the picture. The room around her dimmed...

*****

"Look, Truly!" Geena demanded. "Edgar is doing magic tricks for you. You could show some manners and give him your attention."

"That's okay, honey," Edgar said. "Maybe they aren't good enough. I might not be cut out to be a clown."

"Truly!" Geena yelled.

"I like your tricks," she answered.

"And," Geena said, tapping her foot.

"And maybe you can teach me how to make the coin disappear," Truly mumbled.

"Do you like that one?" Edgar asked.

Truly nodded, keeping her gaze to the floor.

"Okay, sweetheart," Edgar said. "I'll teach you this afternoon. It's not hard to master."

"Are you sure you two will be okay with me working a double shift at the bar?" Geena asked, already at the door with purse in hand. She kissed her fingers then blew on her palm.

"Yeah," Edgar answered. "We are going to have a lot of fun learning new things, aren't we?"

A single tear cascaded down her pink cheeks as the door closed, sealing her fate for another night.

"I tell you what," Edgar said. "I'll teach you how to do the trick first." He winked. "You'll catch on quickly, I'm sure."

Truly sucked in her bottom lip, worrying about what could happen if she didn't.

*****

Truly found herself hunched over the toilet again. This time, dry heaves were all she could manage. Sitting on the cold tile floor, she rested her back against the vanity. She glanced down. A hoarse chuckle escaped her throat. A single coin had somehow found its way into her hand. A snap of her fingers and it disappeared. At least parts of the vision had been true. She still remembered how to do the magic trick.

Chapter Seven

"Anything special on the menu today?" Truly asked, tying a frilly white apron over top of her pink uniform. She'd managed to squeeze into it for another weekend, swearing to herself as always it would be the last time.

"Hey!" Al yelled, pointing a spatula at her through a serving window. "The collar is done up too far. You know how the uniform is supposed to be worn."

"I'm serving food, not my breasts," Truly argued.

"Wear the uniform properly or take the weekend off!" Al ordered.

Truly mumbled a few choice words under her breath while unzipping the front of her one-piece ensemble. It was bad enough it barely covered her ass. Showing off cleavage as well seemed like overkill for a coffee shop.

"I heard that," Al smirked. "Get to work."

"There's no customers, yet," Maria complained. "What are we supposed to do?"

"Try dancing on the tables," Al ordered. "Maybe some will come in then."

"Pig," Maria scoffed. "You are lucky your other jobs have nice bosses."

"Lucky," Truly huffed. "My ass of a landlord more than makes up for that. He actually said I could work off the extra rent in his bed."

"O-M-G!" Maria replied. "He didn't. What did you say?"

"What do you mean, what did I say?!" Truly shrieked. "No, of course."

"I was just asking," Maria muttered. "Making rent is kinda a big deal. I'm sure you've considered..."

"No!" Truly interrupted. "I'm not considering that. I'll find another way. Maybe I'll have to cut back on my doctor appointments to twice a month."

"You see," Maria stated, wagging a finger at her co-worker. "You should have come with me to the psychic thing. All the answers were waiting to be found."

"I doubt any of my answers were there," Truly mumbled.

"You are too negative," Maria blurted out. "Here. I brought you back a fortune telling kit."

Truly flashed a skeptical eye. "A what?" she smirked, taking the package. "What is all this?"

"It has all sorts of do-it-yourself future telling aids," Maria explained. "The first one is a form of paper folding... I forget the name."

"Origami?" Truly questioned, one eyebrow arching.

Maria snapped her fingers. "That's it. Then there's the pen. When you click it, a different message appears on the side."

"What's in the box?" Truly asked.

"That's a really neat one," Maria replied, rubbing her hands together. It's a cloudy sphere. When you shake it, the mist clears and a message floats before your eyes. You can literally ask it anything and it answers."

"Great," Truly said, nodding.

"You don't like it?" Maria asked.

"No, it's great. Thank you," Truly answered, wiping down the same counter for the fifth time. "I don't like this stuff much. I think I'm more of the unfortunate type."

"That's truly unfortunate," Maria snorted.

"What's going to be truly unfortunate is what will happen to my two waitresses if one of them doesn't serve the only customer we have!" Al barked.

"Oh no," Maria snarled, turning up her top lip, "Its Earl. Isn't it your turn..."

"Yeah, yeah," Truly replied, heading over with a menu and the coffee pot. "What can I get you?" She pulled a pencil from behind her ear.

"That uniform is looking mighty nice on you," Earl said, a lopsided grin forming. "Your butt looks firm enough to eat off of. Is that an option here?" He reached around and swatted her.

"Hey!" Truly complained. "No, it's not an option. Keep your hands to yourself."

"Well then, I guess I'll have the usual and a coffee," Earl said. "Make it to go. Al, you got to teach these young fillies some manners. The customer is always right."

"I keep telling them," Al replied, shaking his head. "They don't listen much."

"Hey, Earl," Maria called out. "What's your sign?"

"I'm a Virgo," Earl replied. "Why, you matching us in the stars, beautiful?"

Maria chuckled, shoving the horoscope section of the paper in front of her friend.

Truly grabbed the newspaper. "You should read this, Earl. There's some good advice in it." She circled the entry for his sign in red ink.

He walked up to the counter to pick up his order, taking the circulating column at the same time. He snorted, reading it out loud. *"Be wary of angering women today. It is best for your own health to keep a safe distance..."*

"You two think that's funny?" Al asked, his spatula shaking at them.

"That's okay," Earl said, tossing payment down on the counter. "That's for the food. And this..." He waved a bill in the air, his phone number written across the front. "Is for you." He shoved it into Truly's cleavage, laughing.

"Hey," Truly complained, but it was too late. Earl was already out the door. She stood frozen on the spot, wondering what had just happened.

"Did you see that, Al?" Maria complained, rubbing her co-worker's back. "That wasn't showing off a little skin to keep you in business. Earl groped your employee. What are you going to do about it?"

"Fine," Al replied, throwing his arms in the air. "I'll have a word with one of my only patrons. Then, when nobody comes through the door, none of us will have a job." The spatula landed in the sink with a clang. "Go sit down, Truly. Take a break for a bit. There's nothing to do anyways."

"Go on," Maria agreed. "I'll be right there with a hot tea. You want milk?"

Truly nodded. Milk was a luxury when one didn't have a fridge - a lot of things were. Her mind raced, going over all the things should have said and done. It was easy to think of them now that it was over. Her hand smacked her forehead. Why didn't she at least slap his face?

Steam rose from the glass as it slid in front of her. Her eyes glossed over, watching the liquid swirling...

*****

"What's that?" Priscilla squawked.

"It's a bunch of buttercups," Truly answered. "They are for my show-and-tell."

"That's not real show-and-tell items," Priscilla argued. "My father gave me this necklace." She held out a golden heart with a shiny stone in the middle. "That's a real diamond. He bought it for me so I had something nice for show-and-tell."

"That's nice," Truly mumbled, holding her gaze on the tiny bouquet in her hand.

"What makes you think you can bring in a handful of weeds?" Priscilla questioned.

"They aren't weeds," Truly argued. "I already told you they are buttercups. You hold them under your chin. If a soft yellow glow appears, it means you like butter. If it doesn't... you don't."

"Give me those," Priscilla demanded, grabbing the flowers. "I bet it always makes you look yellow." She held a few up to her chin, letting the rest fall to the ground. "Am I glowing?"

"No!" Truly yelled. "You don't like butter. You don't like anything. Give them back."

A fire erupted in Priscilla's gaze. She dropped the remaining flowers on the ground, the heel of her shoe grinding them into the ground.

"I happen to like butter," Priscilla announced, sticking her nose in the air. "Your stupid weeds lied." She turned and skipped away.

Tears dripped off Truly's perfectly round face, landing on the pile of smashed buttercups. She sniffled. Those flowers were the only thing she had for show-and-tell. How could she face the rest of her class?

"I saw some growing by the forest," Jeffrey said. "If you hurry, you could pick another bunch and still make it back before the bell rings."

"Thanks," Truly replied, wiping her nose with her sleeve. Her feet moved faster than they ever had before.

Students weren't allowed to enter the forest that bordered the school grounds. Just past the first trees, she could see the tiny yellow flowers growing in a bunch. She hurried in to pick them. A bell sounded in the background.

*****

Truly glanced up. What she heard hadn't been a bell, it was sirens passing by outside. She knelt on the padded bench seat, trying to find a better vantage point to see what was going on.

Maria headed back from the door. "Someone was hit crossing the road. I hope they are okay."

Chapter Eight

"How do we end up with all the crap calls?" Jeff complained. His cup almost made it to his lips before the lid fell off, dumping coffee all over his pants. "Ow! Damn!"

"Don't drink and drive," Miranda snickered. "That's my motto." She handed him a few napkins. "And we get all the crap calls because of all your weird ideas. I swear your brain is lost in the clouds somewhere. I don't even know where you come up with some of your scenarios. I can tell you one thing, though... we won't be detectives for long if you keep it up."

"Some partner you are," Jeff scoffed. "You're supposed to have my back." He parked the car at the side of the road. The napkins offered little help removing the wet spot left behind as a reminder of the coffee he didn't have a chance to drink. With a new case waiting, there was no time to worry about either issue. After the preliminary investigation was through, he could grab a dry pair of pants and another caffeine fix, not necessarily in that order.

"I do have your back," Miranda argued, lifting the yellow police tape to duck under. "But let's look at this one as a simple accident. Not everything is murder. If you keep trying to make it one, we'll both have our asses busted back to walking the beat."

"Fine," Jeff agreed, throwing his hands in the air in defeat. "We'll do it your way... for now. I can't overlook evidence, though... and I don't expect you to ask me to."

Miranda rolled her eyes at her partner. "What we got, Sergeant?" she asked. "Open and shut accident, I hope." She glanced under a sheet at the mangled body. "Wow! He must have been hit at full speed to sustain that much damage."

"His name is Earl... forty-three years old, construction worker, and single," the officer stated. "It appears he wasn't watching where he was going and stepped out in front of oncoming traffic. You beat the coroner here."

"What would cause a man to not notice he was about to step in front of a moving vehicle?" Jeff questioned. "He'd have to be deep in thought to completely miss what was going on around him."

"It could have been lots of things," Miranda answered. "But if no one pushed him, it's an accident."

"Hm," Jeff hummed, putting on a pair of latex gloves.

"Oh no," Miranda groaned. "I know that tone. The guy stepped into traffic on his own, Jeff. There is no foul play about that. Let's leave it that way."

"She's right, Detective," the Sergeant agreed. "He had a coffee in one hand and his phone in the other."

"Who was he texting?" Jeff questioned, examining the deceased. "What could be that important..."

A glove smacked against Miranda's skin. She picked up the phone. "The screen is cracked, but I can still read it." She chuckled. "He was sexting some girl."

"Sexting?" Jeff asked, raising an eyebrow.

"Yeah," Miranda replied. "Lots of hot stuff about what they wanted to do to each other. That's enough to keep any guy's attention. What's that?"

"Today's horoscopes," Jeff answered, the frown lines on his face deepening. "You got ID for this guy, Sergeant?"

"Sure," the officer replied.

"Do me a favour, take a look and tell me what sign he was," Jeff requested.

"Sign?" the officer echoed.

"Astrological sign," Jeff explained. "Capricorn, Libra, Gemini, Scorpio? We all have one."

Miranda took the wallet from the officer's hand. "Earl was a Virgo."

"Huh," Jeff huffed. "Listen to this... *Be wary of angering women today. It is best for your own health to keep a safe distance.*"

"Guess he should have listened to the stars," the officer snorted. "Sorry."

"No," Jeff said. "You are right. This was a warning. I think this man was set up."

"Ah, Jeff," Miranda said through grinding teeth. "Remember what we discussed... not everything is murder."

"I'll keep that in mind," he mumbled. "Anyone know where this coffee came from?"

Miranda slapped the palm of her hand against her forehead. "Here we go again. Why can't you leave it at accident?"

"Because," Jeff answered. "I don't think it was one." He grabbed the wallet. "Look at the guy's picture."

"And..."

"What does his face look like to you?" Jeff asked.

"Like an average, middle-aged guy," Miranda answered. "Okay... he may have had a few more hardships over the years than the next guy. He looks older than his age. What's that got to do with anything?"

"Forty-three year old average single guys don't have girls sexting them," Jeff explained. "Guys like Earl are lucky to see a date. The closest they get to a naked woman is at a strip club, and even then, only if the bill waving in their hand is big enough."

"Okay," Miranda said. "I'll buy that. It doesn't mean he was murdered, though."

Jeff pursed his lips together. "I'll make you a deal," he offered. "We track down the other half of the conversation. If she checks out, it's case closed."

"Deal," Miranda replied. "Until then, no further investigations. I'm not opening a can of worms. The last thing we need is people complaining to the captain."

"Fair enough." Jeff smiled, pulling off his glove. "I could use a coffee. I did spill mine earlier."

"No way we are going near that coffee shop," Miranda snickered.

Jeff laughed. "You can't blame a guy for trying."

Chapter Nine

The bus rolled to a stop in front of the Chinese restaurant. Truly, stood, but was forced to wait as an elderly lady had a few choice words for the driver.

"I don't expect to see you speeding through this neighbourhood again, young man." She wagged a finger in his face. "If I do, I will report you. It isn't safe."

Truly watched the woman descending the stairs one at a time. "What was that about, Stan?"

The driver sighed. "You know as well as I do that I don't usually work this shift," he replied. "Every now and then, someone doesn't show up for work and I end up stuck with a double. My wife works nights. I have to be home in time to watch the kids when she leaves. When I work to ten thirty and she has to be at work by eleven, I have to put the pedal to the metal, so to speak, for everyone to make it to where they need to be in time. It's late and there isn't anyone on this road, anyways."

"You pass right by here on your way home?" Truly asked. "I've never noticed before."

"You probably never would have, if it weren't for that lady," Stan suggested. "I have to go by here at exactly quarter to. It takes me five minutes from here to reach my house. The wife gets exactly ten minutes to get to work."

"That's tight," Truly commented.

"Yeah," Stan replied. "I have zero room for error and no choice in the matter."

"Good luck tonight," Truly offered, exiting the bus. She trotted across the street to the restaurant with only five minutes to spare herself and that was allotted to changing.

"Hey. What's going on in there?" Truly asked, nodding to the private party room. Her fingers added the finishing touches to a black tie, her pink uniform having been traded for a pair of dress pants and crisp white long-sleeved shirt in the bathroom.

"It's my Uncle's birthday," Sheylin answered. "I bet he's getting a lot of funny gifts." she chuckled. "He loves his jokes."

Truly smiled. If there was one thing Mr. Cheung enjoyed, it was a good gag.

"Oh," Sheylin said. "I almost forgot. A large dinner party is coming in and they asked for you to be their server."

"Someone asked for me?" Truly questioned, folding napkins into the shape of little hats. "Who made the reservations?"

"Mr. Bernard Bailey," Sheylin answered. "He was most adamant that you be the only one to wait on his table. Looks like you have an admirer."

Truly's face drained of colour. She offered the best chuckle left in her arsenal. "Great. I can use a good tip," she replied. "If they leave one..."

"I'm sure they will," Sheylin answered. "It would be considered most rude to ask for a server and not leave a sizable tip. Are you okay? You look a bit peckish. Why don't you sit down and have a bowl of soup before we open?"

Truly nodded, adding a *thank you* when the bowl arrived. Her lips puckered, allowing air to pass through to cool the first spoonful. It made little difference, burning her tongue. The spoon swirled around in the liquid...

*****

Truly ignored the first warning bell; there was something much more exciting in front of her. The forest floor resembled a gigantic checkerboard, the type Edgar played games on with his friends some nights. In the centre sat the fanciest chair she'd ever seen.

Her eyes danced with curiosity as she took her place within the comforts of the red velvet seat. Tiny fingers ran over the plush material - the tickling sensation bringing forth a toothy grin accompanied by a high-pitched giggle.

"Does it please you?" a man asked, stepping out of the trees. He went down on one knee before her.

Her smile hid, leaving curiosity remaining to face the stranger alone.

He removed his tall hat, revealing some rather odd features. A long bent nose jutted out above small thin lips. Behind those was an array of metals instead of pearly white teeth. When he turned his head, she could see a ribbon similar to her own tying his dark curly hair back in a tidy bunch.

"I'm not supposed to talk to strangers," Truly whispered. "I should go back to school."

"But you are sad," the man stated. "That girl is mean to you. I've been watching."

"Why?" Truly asked.

"I don't like bullies," he answered. "My name is Damionion. And this is my palace." Even standing, he remained somewhat hunched over.

"Onion." Truly giggled. "Like the vegetable?"

The man roared with warm laughter. "Exactly like the onion. I want to help you, Truly."

"How can you help me?" she questioned. "The teacher won't let you on school grounds."

"No," the man agreed, tapping a crooked finger against his snout. "But I could give you a gift." He flapped the long tails of his jacket behind him.

"A gift," she echoed.

Damionion snapped his fingers and a paper fortune teller game appeared in his hand. "This is for you," he offered. He attempted to straighten using a black cane to push up on.

"What is it?" Truly questioned, tilting her head, her small hands unsure if they should touch the elegantly decorated folded paper.

"It's a game," the man revealed. "You use two fingers and both of your thumbs in the corners like this." He demonstrated how to open and close it, keeping two corners together and the other two separated at all times. "Then ask any question you want to know the answer to."

"Will I ever meet my dad?" Truly blurted out.

The man smiled. "Now pick a number." He held the paper fortune teller in front of her nose.

"Um," Truly hummed. "Six!"

Damionion counted to six as he opened and closed the device. "Pick another number."

Truly examined her choices. "One."

The man lifted the corner of the paper with the number one on it and read the message underneath. "Yes!" he exclaimed.

"Yes what?" Truly asked, scrunching up her nose.

"Yes, you will meet your father," Damionion stated. "That was your original question, wasn't it?"

She nodded.

"That calls for a celebration." He stood, raising his arms in the air. Red flower petals rained down around them.

Truly giggled. "I wish I could stay here with you," she said, a pout forming on her lips.

"I do too," the man answered. "But you can't. Perhaps when you are older, you'll make that decision. Today, however, you have a show-and-tell to attend."

"Can I use the paper game?" Truly asked.

The man pursed his lips together. "I think it is best you use the buttercups. This device is special. You can share it with your friends at recess."

"Priscilla will just ruin it," she stated.

"Hm." He tapped a finger against the side of his head. "I want you to offer it to her. Let her see her future. If you do that, I can take care of everything else. Okay?"

"Okay," Truly agreed, the smile returning. Any fear she felt from first meeting the man had vanished. "I should go now. I'm already late. I could get in trouble."

"No, you won't," the man said, smiling. "The bell is only just about to ring. Hurry."

She turned back. "Will I see you again?"

"Anytime you need my help," he said, replacing his hat. "I'm only a fortune away."

****

"Truly!" Sheylin called out. "Are you okay?"

Truly shook her head, erasing the lingering fuzz. "Sorry," she mumbled, still gaining her bearings. "I've been feeling a little off. How long until we open?"

"Five minutes ago," Sheylin answered. "Your tables are filling up."

"Right," Truly said, grabbing an order pad and pencil. "Sorry. I'm ready."

The first tables of the night were relatively easy. The majority of people who came to a buffet ordered water to save extra expense. That meant the only work for her was clearing dishes off of tables throughout the evening. Bernard Bailey's group showed up an hour later.

A wave of relief washed over her, bringing with it the colour her face had previously lost. The table's drink order might have been substantial, but it also came without an ounce of harassment. Fears of being stalked by her landlord subsided when she realized she was serving a family gathering.

Letting her guard down, however, turned out to be a huge mistake on her part. She felt his clammy grip through the material of her shirt, pulling her into a corner.

"Is there a problem, sir?" she asked, trying to remain on a waitress-customer level.

"There is," Bernard answered. "That outfit hides your cute butt a little too well." He squeezed her behind, a grin smothering his face. "Have you made your decision?"

"I'm working," she replied.

"I expect an answer tonight," he said, chuckling. "You know the number."

"And if I don't give you one?" Truly questioned.

"The price goes up," Bernard answered, playing with a strand of her hair. "Remember the two guys who moved your appliances out. They agreed to forgo their bill in lieu of a piece of your ass. Your choice... have me or have three." He grabbed a plate, filling it to the point of bits falling off the sides before returning to his table.

A silver pitcher shook in her grasp as she poured a glass of ice water. Chugging it back, she successfully suppressed the urge to vomit. Making it through the rest of the evening relied on not having any more one-on-one contact with Bernard Bailey.

"Can I get you anything else?" Truly asked, clearing the last of the dishes from their table. Other patrons had long since vacated the premises.

"No, thank you," a younger man answered, offering a warm smile. "Just the check."

Truly returned the smile. It made sense someone other than Bernard was footing the bill. She placed the white slip on the table face-down. Holding a silver tray of fortune cookies, she offered one to each of the group, presenting the final one to her landlord.

"Thank you for your business," she added, heading to the backroom. Her shift had already ended and bed was calling her name.

Chapter Ten

"We've been trying to get in touch with you," Doctor Stevenson said without looking up from his paperwork.

"Sorry," Truly mumbled. "My phone bill... I was late paying it. I've been using a pay-as-you-go one until they switch my service back on. Did I miss a hypnosis session?"

"No," the doctor replied. "But you might have. In future, you need to keep us up-to-date on how to contact you. My colleague, Doctor Sven, happens to be here today. We've set up a control room for your regression to take place in. I'll need you to sign this release."

Truly glanced over the papers. "What are these for?" she questioned.

"The reason why these sessions are free for you," he explained. "Doctor Sven and I are collaborating on research for a new study. This paper lets us release the results of your sessions... otherwise we couldn't use it. There's the whole patient-doctor confidentiality thing professionals have to worry about."

"So you want to tell people I am crazy," Truly mumbled.

"No!" Doctor Stevenson exclaimed, chuckling. "We want to use the data of your case to draw conclusions. We have no intentions of using your name."

"No intentions," Truly echoed, "but you could."

He pursed his lips together, nodding. "It is a general release," he agreed. "Theoretically, I suppose we could, but that isn't the plan. If you would prefer to pay for the program, it can be arranged. I must warn you, though... Doctor Sven is much more expensive than I am."

"If you can include our regular sessions without charge, I'd be willing to sign," Truly blurted out.

"You are quite the negotiator," the doctor answered. "I think that can be arranged." He held up a black pen with gold trim. "Sign on the dotted line and we can begin."

Truly sucked in her top lip, allowing her teeth to graze over it. Her gaze alternated between the fancy pen and the white paper as she weighed her options. Without medical bills, making rent seemed an attainable goal and she wouldn't need to consider taking Bernard Bailey's offer. In the end, she traded one evil for the other. Being embarrassed in front of others was easier to handle than being embarrassed of one's self. The ink flowed smoothly, sealing yet another deal with the devil.

"Excellent," Doctor Stevenson praised, snatching both the paper and pen back. "Is there anything you'd like to discuss before we go meet Doctor Sven?"

Truly's mind screamed yes, but her body had other plans. Her head shook, lips remaining sealed.

"Are you sure?' he pried.

Her eyes fell upon a cellophane bag peeking out of her purse. She'd all but forgotten about the package of future predictors. "Thank you," she blurted out. "For the free sessions. I'd like to give you a gift. It's not much, but I think you might enjoy it." She pulled out the small box. "It makes predictions when you shake it."

"That's very thoughtful," her doctor replied. "It looks fascinating." Without opening the package, it disappeared into a bottom drawer of his desk. "Shall we?" He stood, motioning for her to follow him.

Chapter Eleven

"What we got?" Jeff asked, ducking under the yellow caution tape.

"Another accident," the responding officer replied. "He walked right out in front of an off-route bus."

"Witnesses?" Miranda questioned.

"Loads," the officer replied. "His whole family was out to dinner at a buffet." He pointed at the restaurant. "They confirm he stepped off the curb and wham."

"Identification?" she questioned.

"Bernard Bailey, age fifty-two and divorced," the officer stated. "Another case of texting and crossing the road." He held up a cell phone already bagged as evidence.

"That's two in as many days," Jeff commented.

"Accidents happen," Miranda said. "People need to leave their phones at home."

"Any clue who he was texting?" Jeff questioned. "Another sexting session, by chance?"

"Not this time," the officer answered. "There was only one word on the phone... *okay*. It looks like he never had the chance to reply. Maybe that's what he was about to do when he was hit."

Jeff scowled, squatting beside the body. "Hand me a glove, will ya?" he said, holding one hand behind him.

"Did you find something?" Miranda asked.

"I can see a small piece of paper in one hand," he replied. "Some tweezers would be great."

His partner handed him his requests, peeking over his shoulder at the deceased's clenched fist. "He's already started stiffening. You might not get that out until the autopsy... at least, not intact."

Jeff grunted his reply, the tweezers tugging hard on the scrap. In the end, the icy grip of death won out. Whatever the man was clinging to, it was of no good to them in little bits.

"It's an accident," Miranda stated. "I'm going to get a statement from the restaurant owners and family. You can wait for the body pick up."

"Thanks," Jeff replied, smiling. "I have a couple questions for the coroner anyways."

"Accident," Miranda called out, heading towards the last place anyone saw the man alive.

*****

"I need to ask a few questions for our file," Miranda stated, glancing at worried faces. "It's standard procedure when a death happens. If you'd all take a seat, I'll get to each of you as quickly as possible."

"There was nothing suspicious," a white-haired lady blurted out. "He wasn't watching where he was going."

"You are?" Miranda asked.

"His mother," she replied in a matter-of-fact tone. "It serves him right. Karma always comes back to kick a fool in the pants. I've said it for years. When he got that fortune, I knew it was coming for him. Of course, I didn't think it would be quite so soon."

"Fortune?" Miranda questioned, glancing up from her notes. "What fortune?"

"From the cookie," she stated. "It foretold his demise, in black and white."

"A fortune cookie with a bad fortune in it..." Miranda mumbled to herself. "I didn't know such a thing existed."

"Oh, yes," Mr. Cheung answered. "They are called unfortunate cookies." He chuckled. "Very funny."

"And you serve these to your customers?" Miranda inquired, her eyebrows arched.

"No." Mr. Cheung shook his head. "That would be bad business."

"Then how did Mr. Bailey end up with one?" Miranda questioned. "Do you keep any in the restaurant?"

"Not normally," Sheylin answered. "Tonight was my uncle's birthday. He received some as a gift. I have no idea how one would end up in a customer's possession, though."

"Who knew about the unfortunate cookies?"

"Myself," Sheylin answered, "the family and possibly the staff. Everyone who has met my uncle knows he finds little pranks amusing."

"Is this everyone who was working?" Miranda continued her questioning.

"Yes," Sheylin answered. "Except for one waitress. Truly left before the accident happened. She wasn't feeling well most the night and Mr. Bailey's table was the last to finish eating."

"I'll need her name and contact information," the detective stated. "Was there anything else odd about the night?"

"Just one thing," Sheylin admitted. "When the table was booked, Mr. Bailey requested Truly as his server by name. That never happens."

"Thank you," Miranda offered, snapping her notebook closed. I'll send an officer in to collect contact information."

"Can we go, then?" Mrs. Bailey asked.

"As soon as the officer has your numbers, yes," she replied, heading for the door. Her notepad slapped against the palm of her opposite hand with every step. Jeff was going to have a field day with the similarities between the two accidental deaths. She wasn't sure if it was murder, but something strange was happening in Knollville.

Chapter Twelve

Apprehension grabbed her nerves from the moment the silver door handle turned. She hadn't even realized there was another part to the medical facility before, Doctor Stevenson's office being the only room she'd visited past the reception desk. Now she wished she hadn't found out.

The hypnosis room was actually a seclusion cell. It might as well have been padded and her confined within a straightjacket. A single reclining chair stole the focus of anyone entering - the type one might expect to find in a dentist's office, including the mint green colour.

"Doctor Sven," Stevenson said, "I'd like to introduce your new patient, Truly."

"A pleasure," the man said, extending his hand.

Doctor Stevenson's colleague was a white man in his forties. Many a woman would have killed to have his naturally bleach blonde hair and curls. A slight accent indicated he was from a European background, although she wasn't sure exactly which country he hailed from.

Truly matched his offering with her own hand. "It's nice to meet you," she mumbled, still apprehensive about the room. From the white linoleum tile to the plain walls, it was the definition of bland. This was a place where dreams were destroyed and minds broken. There was no fixing in the equation.

"Please have a seat. I want you to be comfortable and relax," Dr. Sven said. "I need you to remove your sweater, shoes and socks."

She alternated glances between the two doctors. Relaxing was easier said than done in a room completely void of signs of existence. Realizing, to the men before her, silence was an indication of an inner struggle with herself, she complied. A motor hummed as the chair reclined without any effort on her part.

"You are tense," Doctor Sven commented. "Don't worry. This won't hurt. I will mention a few things before we begin. I will be putting you into a hypnotic state, during which time you will have no recollection of the events that occur. For your safety, there are cameras recording the entire session. You are free to look at the sessions at any time. The footage will also allow Doctor Stevenson and myself to go over the results at a later date without relying on memory. As we all know, there are three sides to every tale and we want only the truth to use for your treatment and our data. Okay?"

Truly nodded, licking her lips. If the speech had been meant to ease her mind, it failed miserably. She hadn't considered the possibility that something could happen to her body while her mind was preoccupied before.

"First, I need to attach these electrodes to you in order to monitor vital information. That will allow me to ensure you are safe at all times. If any of the signals are outside of the norm, we'll pull you back to a conscious state."

Truly grimaced at the abrasive lotion being applied to her skin, followed by a cold sensation and round patches connected to wires. She groaned as tape went over top to hold each in place. She didn't need a mirror to know she looked more like a lab rat than a person, especially with cords running from her ankles, chest and head to a device she couldn't even see. There was also a clamp that locked on one finger. From behind, she could hear the clicks of connections being made to presumably some form of monitor. All the added stress was going to make it difficult for her to follow Doctor Sven's instructions about relaxing.

"Good!" The hypnosis specialist said, with a thunderous clap of his hands. "Let's get this show on the road. Close your eyes. I'm going to describe a scene and I want you to picture it and hear it in your mind as if it were happening directly in front of you."

She chuckled. That was easier said than done. Squirming her body around, she found the most comfortable position possible without disrupting any of the technology she had been hooked up to. "Okay," she said, adding a sigh.

"Don't worry," Doctor Sven suggested. "I know what I am doing. You'll be fine. Now close your eyes and listen to my voice."

What else am I going to do? she thought.

"Clear your mind completely," the doctor said, his voice becoming softer. "When you are free of all the burdens of this world, I want you to tell me your favourite word... one that rolls off your tongue and is fun to say. When you have it, tell me."

"Mahogany," Truly answered. Not only was the word fun, but the wood itself was one of her favourites. Its deep and rich colour warmed her, especially in antique items.

"Mahogany," the doctor repeated, letting each letter roll off his tongue, flowing into the next. "I want you to imagine a room built entirely in mahogany... the floor... the walls... the furniture."

Truly's heart skipped a beat. The vision forming was a dream come true. This was the place she wanted to live the rest of her life in.

"I'm going to count backwards from ten," the doctor said, his voice nothing more than a background noise. "At every number, you'll receive a mahogany box to open. Inside is something that comforts you... relaxes you. As you open each, you will release more and more of the stress and inhibitions that bind you to the conscious, relaxing further and drifting into a deep sleep. Ten."

Truly sat cross-legged in the middle of her mahogany dream. A box similar to a picnic basket appeared before her. She pulled the handles on the top. Ten bright green balloons escaped, floating upwards. She felt a comfortable numbness taking over her fingers and toes as each drifted towards the sky. For the first time, she realized there was no ceiling to her perfect room.

"Watch the tension escape from your body," the doctor's voice hummed gently. "With each passing number, you will become more and more relaxed. When I reach the number one, you will be fully asleep, but continue to hear my voice. Nine."

A new box appeared before her. Her fingers twitched, eager to see the contents. Nine brightly coloured butterflies fluttered out, each performing a dance choreographed for her eyes only, before drifting away to join the balloons. Her breathing slowed, all apprehension beginning to dissipate.

"With each passing number, all the worries of everyday life fade away," the doctor continued. "As you relax, you feel your eyelids becoming heavy. Each box brings you closer to a state of total sleep. You will continue to hear and respond to my voice, but remain asleep until I awake you with your chosen word. Eight."

A new box brought anticipation. Her hands, numbed by tranquility, still moved upon command, releasing eight plastic kites with long tails of material shaped in triangles. A gust of wind blew them from side to side before lifting them away into a clear blue sky. Truly felt a sigh roll off of her tongue as it too shared in her newfound peacefulness.

"Your body is becoming lighter as you drift further into a deep sleep, hearing only the sound of my voice," Doctor Sven continued while monitoring a screen of incoming data. "Seven."

Truly smiled, a new box appearing within her reach. This time, seven bubbles floated out. The perfectly formed iridescent spheres wobbled, bumping into each other as they escaped to serenity.

"You can feel anxiety and worries lifting off your shoulders with each container opened. Your body is becoming weightless. Six."

A new wooden crate appeared. Her hands moved in slow motion, grasping the handles to reveal its secrets. Six white doves cooed before majestically soaring to the skies.

Doctor Sven pulled over a stool on wheels to sit on, removing a hidden tray from the backside of the chair. "As each number passes, you become more and more tired, relaxation flowing through you as blood pumps through your veins. Five."

Truly glanced around, a fogginess taking over her senses. She glanced at the next box, willing her hands to open it, but they no longer responded. It opened nonetheless, releasing five puffs of white smoke. She watched them grow as they rose, forming fluffy clouds in the sky above.

"Your body has become completely weightless. You have no desire to open your eyes as you drift further into sleep with every offering. Four."

Not even grogginess could stop her from willing the next box to open. She yearned for the peaceful contentment it contained. A single dandelion grew from inside. Its life cycle went into overdrive, from the bloom of the yellow weed to its transformation into cottony seeds. Making one wish for each of the four, she puckered her lips, her breath releasing them. As they floated upwards, they took with them bits of remaining tension from her limbs.

"Your eyelids are too heavy to open now," the doctor said, pressing a few buttons on the monitor. "You are drifting further into sleep, but will continue to hear the sound of my voice. I will be a beacon to you; a lifeline to hold on to. You fully understand you are completely safe. A simple tug and I'll pull you away from any danger. Three."

Truly watched three perfectly-folded paper airplanes circle her before taking off to their new destination. Her mind smiled, her face too relaxed to move.

"Relaxation washes over you," the doctor said, his voice lower and softer than before. "You feel safe in perfect tranquility, ready to explore your own psyche. Two."

Truly's pupils followed two bumblebees as they buzzed before her, their wings moving in slow motion. The fogginess of sleep thickened as they disappeared upwards.

"At the end of the countdown, you will be completely asleep," the doctor said. "You will still hear my voice and respond to it. You fully understand nothing here can hurt you. You are safe. One."

The final box opened, releasing a single particle of dust. It floated in slow motion upwards, vanishing as quickly as it appeared.

"You are now completely asleep," Doctor Sven stated, pulling out a pencil and notebook. "When you hear your chosen word, you will wake up feeling completely refreshed and with no memories of any events. Raise your right arm if you understand."

Truly's arm lifted.

"Good." he said. "You can lower it now."

The arm fell back in place at her side.

"I want you to go back in time to let me speak to a nine-year-old Truly," the doctor explained. "Tell me your name and age."

"Truly DeCanter," her voice squeaked. "I'm almost ten."

The two doctors exchanged glances, scribbling down the last name.

"Can you tell me where you live?" The doctor questioned.

"Geena and I moved into Edgar's house," Truly answered. "She says it is best for us."

"Who is Geena?" the doctor pried.

"She's my mother, but she prefers I don't tell anyone that," Truly replied. "She says she is too young to be a mom and folks will think we are sisters that way."

The doctor shook his head. "I see," he commented. "Is Edgar your father?"

"No," Truly said, a childhood pout forming on her lips. "I heard them talking about my father. They said he was a crooked man that abandoned me. That's how Geena got stuck taking care of me."

"How do you feel about that?"

Truly paused for a moment, letting out a huff. "I wish he was here to look after me... things would be better then."

"What things?" the doctor pried. A series of bells went off on the monitor.

A frown joined the pout on Truly's face. "I'm not allowed to talk about that."

"Okay," the doctor agreed. "You don't have to." He watched her levels return to normal before continuing. "Did anything odd happen at school?"

Truly saw her mahogany room transform into a familiar scene. The wooden floors were replaced with checkerboard white and black tiles. Trees and bushes lined the edges, forming natural walls. Her body floated to the comfortable red cushions of the single throne-like chair. She glanced down, admiring the wine-coloured satin dress that had replaced her jeans and t-shirt.

"There was a man," she said, her voice no longer that of a child.

The doctor put down his pad of paper. "What man?"

"A magic man," she replied, a grin crossing her face. "He was tall, but curves made him normal-sized."

"Curves?" the doctor questioned.

"He was off-centre when he stood. His nose was long and bent as well," Truly explained.

"You said he was a magic man, can you explain?" the doctor pried. "Did he do tricks?"

"No," Truly said, chuckling. "Edgar did tricks. He taught me how to make a coin disappear once. This man controlled real magic. He said he would take away all my problems."

"And did he?" the doctor asked.

"He did," Truly replied.

"What did you have to do for him?" the doctor asked.

"Nothing," Truly stated. "Other than handing people their fortunes. He handled the rest."

"What did he do?"

"He made sure their fortunes came true." Truly said. "Once they looked at it, their fates were sealed."

"And were any of the fortunes bad?" the doctor pried.

"Yes," Truly admitted.

"Can you give me an example?"

"Edgar received the ace of spades," Truly said. "His house burned down with him in it."

"Did he die?" the doctor asked.

"He did," Truly admitted. "I was there. The only reason I survived is because the man told me to leave."

"Is your mother alive?" the doctor asked.

"No," Truly admitted. "She died right after that."

"Did the man kill her too?"

"Yes," Truly answered. "Even though I didn't see it happen, I know he was responsible."

"What was the man's name?" the doctor questioned. "Do you know?"

"Damionion," Truly stated.

"Do you still see him?" Doctor Sven asked.

"I didn't for a long time, but over the past week, he has been coming around again," Truly replied. "I didn't understand who was talking to me until today. I didn't remember him."

"But now you do?" the doctor asked, exchanging glances with his colleague. "What is your name and how old are you?"

"Truly Alaney and I'm twenty-four years old."

"What does Damionion tell you?" he questioned.

"If anyone hurts me, I only need give them a fortune and he'll take care of them," Truly answered.

Chapter Thirteen

"The fortune came back," Jeff said, walking into his office. He pushed his partner's feet off their combined desk. *"Death comes for those who refuse to change.* It's a rather cryptic message for a cookie."

"We already knew the owner was celebrating a birthday and received a container of unfortunate cookies," Miranda stated, paying no direct attention to him.

"The phone numbers match," Jeff stated, tossing a file down. "Whoever was sexting Earl also sent the message to Bernard. That makes a connection."

Miranda sighed. "That doesn't make it murder. Both cases have witnesses who saw the victims step into traffic of their own accord. No one pushed them or forced them. How do you plan to make a charge stick?"

"This is what I think," Jeff explained. "The fortunes were threats. The calls were distractions. Whoever was on the other end of them, knew the two men would be crossing a street and self-absorbed by their phones."

"Except," Miranda argued, pointing a pencil at her partner, "the horoscope was printed in the paper for everyone to read."

"It was circled in red," Jeff replied. "Somebody gave it to him that way."

"And the fortune cookie?" Miranda inquired. "The whole family made the same statement. They were allowed their choice of cookies. That makes Bernard's a random chance. Anyone at that table could have ended up with it."

"I haven't figured that part out yet," Jeff admitted. "But I will. The phone number is a dead end. It was a non-traceable throw-away."

"Why can't you let this go?" Miranda asked. "We have people to answer to and they are starting to talk."

"Do we care?" Jeff asked, side-eyeing his partner. "Isn't what we do about the truth?"

"It is, but wasting resources on open-and-shut accident cases is garnering a bit of attention," Miranda explained. "Not the good sort, either. We could end up in the unemployment line."

Jeff rubbed the stubble forming on his chin. "I can go it alone," he suggested. "If you want to bail, I understand."

"I'm not jumping ship," Miranda replied. "I just need to be on the same page as you. Why are you so sure these two cases are murders?"

"Because I've seen it before," Jeff admitted. "When I was a kid. My mom and dad joked they were the unfortunate deaths. I saw one happen."

"You never mentioned this before," Miranda said, sitting up straight. "How old were you?"

"Nine," Jeff replied. "A classmate named Priscilla walked right into the road in front of an oncoming car. It was a horrific sight. Even now after years of investigations, it still haunts me."

"And the fortune?" Miranda questioned.

Jeff exhaled quickly through his nostrils. "It was show-and-tell day. Priscilla was the class bully. I know... bullying is wrong. When you are a kid, though, it isn't quite so cut and dry. Priscilla was mean, but she also had the best parties and an overabundance of candy to share. Any kid who wasn't friends with her was missing out. That amounted to one down-on-her-luck girl being pushed around. Her dad abandoned her, her mom was a stripper, her step-dad was a bum and she wore clothes too small. I regret..."

"Hindsight," Miranda said. "You were a kid. Like you said, kids see things differently."

"Yeah," Jeff continued. "On that day, Priscilla destroyed the poor girl's show-and-tell... a bunch of buttercups. By afternoon, she came up with a new idea, an origami fortune teller."

"The ones you stick your fingers and thumbs in?" Miranda asked. "I used to love those."

Jeff nodded. "Priscilla demanded to try it at break. Next thing I knew, she was shrieking and running inside. The other girl bent over and picked up the paper game from the ground. The teacher came out in full stride, grabbing it from her hand."

"What did it say?"

"That's the thing, it was all normal responses," Jeff replied. "Priscilla, however, insisted it said she was going to die. I only looked away for a split second."

"You think the girl switched papers?" Miranda asked.

"It's possible," Jeff said. "And if that was the case, the same could have been done to the cookies." He sighed. "After school, Priscilla walked right into traffic. After the dust settled, the other girl was standing on the other side, alone."

"I don't get it," Miranda admitted. "If she was on the other side how could she have caused the death?"

"A bully's behaviour is easy to estimate," Jeff answered. "She could have stuck out her tongue and Priscilla would have jumped to put her in her place."

"So you are saying this girl planned the accident?" Miranda asked.

"Yeah," Jeff answered. "That's what I am saying. There is a grey area there that happens more than we think. If you know human nature, you can predict how someone will act and use it as a weapon."

"What happened to the girl?" Miranda asked.

"I don't know," Jeff admitted. "There were two more accidents right after that. One was her mother; the other the boyfriend. I assume she became a ward of child services."

"What was her name?" Miranda asked.

"Truly," Jeff said.

"You're kidding!" Miranda exclaimed, flipping open her notes.

"No, why?"

"Truly is the name of the waitress who served Bernard Bailey the night of his death," Miranda stated.

"You think they could be the same person?" Jeff asked.

"I think we need to look at some old files," Miranda replied. "We just might have a serial killer on the loose."

"Then you believe me?" Jeff asked, a half-grin shadowing his face.

"I always did," Miranda admitted. "I just don't know how we can prove any of this beyond a shadow of a doubt. Without something substantial, we'll never make a murder charge stick."

"Yeah," Jeff agreed. "Being smart isn't exactly a typical weapon, although, I suppose it should be."

"Don't tell me you want to start an IQ registry," Miranda snorted. "That would get us kicked off the force without a doubt."

Jeff laughed. "No," he said. "But I am curious who the investigating officer was back then. He might be able to shed some more light on the other cases."

"Officer Henry Doogalen," Miranda said. "What would we do without computers?"

"Investigate the old-fashioned way," Jeff suggested, rounding the desk to look over his partner's shoulder, "by looking things up manually. That's why we have paper trails. We might have to anyways." He nodded at the note on the screen. "The files were sealed for some reason."

"Child services, maybe," Miranda suggested.

"Could be."

"So where do we go now?" she asked.

"I think it's time to pay a visit to the captain," Jeff answered. "This should be fun."

Chapter Fourteen

Miranda moved to the side, allowing her partner easy access to the frosted door. Captain Miller wasn't known for his patience. Disturbing him without a good reason wasn't a good choice for one's career on any day. If he was in a foul mood, the odds of being busted to desk duty or worse went up exponentially.

Replying with a glare, Jeff grabbed the knob and entered in one swift motion.

"Knock!" the captain ordered, pointing at the open exit without looking up.

Jeff backed out of the room, mumbling a few choice words after fully closing the door behind him. His knuckle came down hard, leaving behind noticeable vibrations.

Bulletproof glass partitions had become all the rage in government buildings over the past few years. Knollville's police department, however, had a rather limited budget. The result was the installation of the cheapest plastic substitute known to man, hoping no one would notice the difference. The problem was, it didn't take a genius to see the flimsy material would buckle at the mere sight of the barrel of any weapon. These new doors and windows were even less safe than their predecessors had been.

"Come!" the captain bellowed, pretending the first intrusion never happened. "What can I do for you, detectives?" His eyes remained steadfast on the paperwork before him.

Jeff tossed his files down on the desk, covering his superior's work. "We need to discuss these cases," he stated.

The captain froze for a split second before tossing aside his pen and reading the labels on the folders. "What is it now?" he asked, a sigh riding on his words. "Two accidents should be open-and-shut cases. That's why you were assigned to them."

"I realize that, sir," Jeff stated. "But there is more to these than meets the eye. I believe we have a serial killer on the loose in Knollville."

The captain rubbed his face. "From two traffic accidents, you have put together a case for murder? Why does that not surprise me?"

"Not just two, sir," Jeff replied. "There is a link to several accidents in the past as well."

"In the past?" The captain asked, eyeing his two officers. "And you concur?"

"I do," Miranda answered, holding her breath.

"It's all in my report," Jeff interrupted. "After you read it, I believe you will see the obvious connection."

The captain leaned back in his chair, files in hand. He flipped the first one open and scanned the first pages. The paperwork landed with a thud on his desk.

"What is it you want, Jeff?" he asked

"I would like to speak with the officer who headed up the cases fifteen years ago," he replied. "Henry Doogalen."

The captain's face drained of colour. "Henry Doogalen," he repeated with a huff. "I'll arrange it, but..."

"But?" Jeff echoed, his voice hanging on the word as if his life depended on it.

"But," the captain continued, "you are missing something very important in your report. You need to find that before I go sticking my neck on the line."

"And what would that be?" Miranda questioned.

"A motive!" the captain yelled. "For two detectives, it's sloppy work to miss such an obviously important piece of information.

Why do you believe this girl is killing people? All I see in here is that she was a waitress at the restaurant Bernard ate at the night he died. There isn't even a connection between her and the other deceased. What relationship did she have to your two victims? Or perhaps you believe she is randomly picking targets by pulling them out of her ass?"

"No, sir," Miranda answered, offering her partner a glare. She'd been so caught up in the mystery, she'd forgotten the basics. "We'll get it for you."

"Within twenty-four hours," the captain demanded. "Take your files with you. I have enough real cases cluttering up my desk without adding them."

Jeff complied, letting out a breath of air as he exited. "That went well," he smirked, earning him a punch in the arm. "Ow!"

Miranda grabbed one file. "The only way we are going to get through this in a day is if we split up. I've got Earl," she stated. "You handle Bernard."

"Deal," Jeff agreed. "I don't think this will be too difficult. Nowadays, everyone has a motive."

Chapter Fifteen

Miranda glanced at the outside of the coffee shop, shaking her head. "More like greasy spoon," she mumbled, making her way inside. Glancing at the state of the cushion seats in the booths, she opted for a stool at the counter instead.

"Coffee?" Maria offered.

"Please," she replied, flashing a smile and her badge. Normally that combo meant her order would have been on the house and service swift. In here, however, neither appeared to hold any weight.

It would have taken a rather stupid criminal to attempt to rob a place that had no customers. If there was nothing to steal, it wasn't worth taking the chance. Protection wasn't what they needed, from the police or anyone else.

Maria pursed her lips together, arching her eyebrows at the gold badge. "If it were my decision..."

"I need to ask you a few questions," Miranda interrupted, not wanting to embarrass the waitress any further. "It's about the accident that happened up the street."

"Yeah," Maria replied, nodding. "The other day... we saw all the flashing reds go by. It was too far away for us to notice anything else, though."

"Of course," Miranda agreed. "But..."

"What's all this?" Al complained, poking through the opening meant for passing food. "You are tying up my girl. She has work to do." A white beanie-style cap covered his head and any hair he might have had.

Miranda glanced around the empty restaurant. "I can tell, you're way too busy to answer a few questions. How about I have you close up and drag both of you downtown to make official statements?"

"Alright," Al groaned, throwing his arms in the air. "Alright... but you are going to order something first."

"Fine," Miranda agreed, quickly scanning the one-page menu. "A piece of apple pie."

"One deluxe burger combo with a side of fires and a slice of pie coming right up," Al announced. "Hope you don't mind taking care of the bill before we settle into your questions?"

Miranda groaned. This brought new meaning to the phrase *greasing someone's palm.* The thought of how much grease was involved left her wishing she had picked the other dead guy to investigate.

The sizzling in the kitchen had already begun. Even if the food had been healthy, it would have been too much for her to eat alone in one sitting. The fact that it wasn't made the situation even worse. She could already feel the pores on her face sucking up grease. There was no doubt there were blemishes in her future.

An over-flowing plate slid down the counter, coming to a stop directly in front of her. Reaching in her purse, she pulled out a twenty and sat it beside the food.

"I'll pay the bill and tip when we are done," she stated. "You can see I'm good for it." She placed a set of salt and pepper shakers over the money.

"What could we possibly tell you?" Al asked, using his already-stained apron as a cloth for his hands. His muscles flexed every time he wiped them front and back, accentuating an anchor tattoo peeking out from under his short sleeved shirt.

Why the man chose to wear all white to cook in made no sense to her whatsoever. His outfit showed every spill, burn and stain known to man and probably a few scientists would have been interested in studying as well.

"The deceased bought a coffee here the morning of the accident," Miranda stated.

Maria gasped. "Earl?"

"You knew the victim?" Miranda questioned.

"He was a regular here," Al advised. "He came in all the time. I thought he was mad at my girls for giving him a hard time the other day. I never thought he was dead, that's for sure."

"By girls," Miranda said, "I assume you mean your waitresses. Was there a problem that morning?"

"Earl was a problem every day. He was a pig," Maria replied. "He came in here to gawk at the stingy uniforms the boss makes us wear."

"Hey," Al complained. "There's nothing indecent about the uniforms. Everything is covered. It's all legal."

"You have to admit," Miranda argued, "they are a bit revealing for a coffee shop."

"Eh," Al moaned. "I'm doing my best to make ends meet here. I have to attract customers somehow."

"Sounds like you are attracting the wrong type of customers," Miranda replied. "Tell me more about what happened."

"It was a traffic accident!" Al exclaimed. "What does it matter what happened before he left here?"

"It is standard for all deaths to be fully investigated, accident or otherwise," Miranda stated. "We are trying to piece together why he stepped off the curb into oncoming traffic. The information we have are a cup from your establishment and a newspaper open to the horoscopes with the deceased's sign circled in red."

"He was in here that morning," Maria replied. "He was harassing another waitress. I checked his horoscope and found what it said somewhat ironic so I showed it to her. She circled it in red and gave it to him."

"How did he respond?" Miranda asked.

"In a typical Earl fashion... without notice, he stuffed her tip down her cleavage, making sure she felt it, if you know what I mean. He laughed and left. She was shook up... sat in the far booth for most of the rest of the day."

"I should dock her pay for that," Al muttered, through closed teeth.

"Don't you dare!" Maria ordered. "You made her show off her assets in the first place. It's your fault she was groped."

"I'll need her name and address," Miranda said, trying to ignore their ongoing spat.

"Why?!" Maria exclaimed. "Truly has been through enough lately. She was here when the accident happened. There is no way she was involved."

"Truly is her name?!" Miranda asked.

"Yeah," Maria replied. "I think it suits her. It's different."

"Are you friends?"

"Yeah, I suppose," Maria replied. "It's been a while since we went out together. She works three jobs and has a jerk for a landlord. Just the other night I wanted to take her with some friends to see the new psychic in town."

"Did she go with you?" Miranda questioned.

"Nah," Maria admitted. "She said she hates fortune telling in any form. I brought her back an assortment of things, though. That place has everything you could imagine. If you want to know about the future, it's the place to visit. They even have a psychic museum."

"You said her landlord was a jerk," Miranda commented. "Was he doing anything in particular?"

"He's worse than Earl was," Maria stated. "Bernard the bastard." she chuckled.

Miranda shook her head. "Bernard?!"

"I don't see what any of this has to do with Earl's death," Al complained.

"Sorry," Miranda offered. "I suppose we got off-topic. Girl talk tends to get us women in trouble."

Al rolled his eyes. "Are we done?"

"Yeah," Miranda replied, watching the man snatch the twenty from under the shakers without either so much as rocking.

"Hey." Maria complained. "Part of that tip is mine." She turned her attention back to the officer. "Can I get you anything else?"

"A to-go container would be nice. Thank you." Miranda pulled out her phone and dialed. "Jeff, it's me. When you get this message call me back. I have some information and one more place to go. There's a new fortune telling place in town I want to check out." She smiled, accepting the white take-out container from Maria. "I also picked you up a burger and fries. Talk to you later."

Chapter Sixteen

Jeff's knuckles were still red from knocking on Bernard Bailey's door. It made sense that no one was there, but he had hoped to catch a family member sorting through the deceased's belongings. He also hoped his partner was having better luck than he was.

It was time to go back to the drawing board, or in his case, the file. A once-through was bound to provide him with a good place to start. He exhaled, reading the statements from each of the family members. Next were the restaurant staff who offered little more than putting his suspect at the scene. The missing pieces he needed to figure out were how Bernard Bailey knew Truly, and how she could have known the empty bus would have been passing by at precisely the right moment.

His deductive skills went into overdrive. He had their addresses. She was a tenant there. From the state of the building it was easy to ascertain that Mr. Bailey had been a poor landlord. That at least provided a connection between the two. But if being disgruntled about the state of the apartments was motive for murder, he had an entire building of potential suspects. That was a can of worms he wasn't about to open, at least not yet. There was one option remaining. He needed to talk to the bus driver.

Stan Ryder had been suspended from work after the accident until a full investigation had been completed by Knollville's insurance agents. It was unknown if he'd ever drive a bus again, at least in Knoll County. His life had been turned upside down by the accident. If the murder theory was correct, Stan was just as much a victim as Bernard.

Jeff tensed his fist once again. He grumbled to himself under his breath about people needing to invest in doorbells.

"We have one," Stan stated, pointing to a white circle to the left of the door.

Jeff felt the heat rising in his cheeks. He hadn't expected anyone to hear his self-ranting. "Sorry," he offered, loosening his collar.

"Knollville's finest investigative team at work," Stan said. "I feel safer already." He left the door open, retreating inside.

"I'm sorry to disturb you at home," Jeff offered, following the man.

"Disturb," Stan scoffed. "That would presume I was doing something and, as you can see, I am not."

"I understand your frustration," Jeff replied. "I need to ask you a few questions, though."

Stan leaned back, the front two legs of his kitchen chair leaving the ground. "Shoot."

"Did anything unusual happen the day of the accident?" Jeff asked.

"Not that I recall," Stan answered, pursing his lips together. He twisted the cap off a beer. "You want one?"

"No, thank you," Jeff said. "According to your statement, you were on your way home. Why were you taking the bus home? That isn't exactly standard procedure."

"I was wondering if anyone was going to ask that," he scoffed. "I figured the politicians were burying that detail. I already explained to officers the situation at work."

"Situation?" Jeff questioned, not having seen any mention of it in any of the reports he read. "What situation?"

"The turnover rate for bus drivers is higher than any other government job around here," Stan explained. "It doesn't pay well. I'm the only experienced driver they have. Recruits come and go like the wind. When they go, they usually do it without notice, leaving someone, namely me, stuck working their shifts."

"There are laws against drivers working over a certain number of hours in a day," Jeff commented.

"There are," Stan agreed, pointing at the detective with his beer. "But imagine what would happen if a Knollville bus didn't show up for scheduled routes a few times a week."

Jeff shrugged his shoulders. "People would be upset."

"They wouldn't make it to their jobs, to pick up their kids, to their appointments or home from the mall," Stan continued. "There's a whole domino effect and the last ones to be knocked over..."

"Would be those who run Knollville," Jeff stated.

"Bingo," Stan said, gulping back another mouthful of his brew. "So they make exceptions. I agree to finish another driver's route and they agree to let me take the bus home those days. There isn't enough time for me to finish paperwork, log in the bus and get to my car on top of the actual drive. My wife would lose her job. We have two mortgages, five kids, three cats and a dog. We can't afford that. If it happened and we took my employers to court..."

"Domino effect," Jeff stated, nodding.

Stan pulled a piece of paper from his wallet and tossed it on the table. "I have a permit for parking the bus out front. It's all legal. If I am not completely exhausted, I pack the kids into the bus and return it that evening, fetching my car at the same time. If not, it waits until morning when my wife comes home."

"Thanks for explaining," Jeff said. "Will you be taking action against your employers now?"

Stan's mouth twitched from side to side. "I doubt it. They had to suspend me for the accident to save face. They'll hire me back when things cool down and I'll ask for a sizable raise."

Jeff nodded, knowing that was how most governing authorities functioned. "Did anyone else know the route you were taking that evening?"

"Yeah," Stan replied. "A bus load of passengers knew thanks to one old broad who caught a glimpse of me speeding home one night."

"You wouldn't happen to know any names of the passengers at the time, would you?" Jeff inquired.

"I don't get why you would want to know that," Stan declared. "What good would it do in an accident investigation? The guy stepped into the street in front of me. I hit him. Case closed."

"Humour me," Jeff requested.

"Fine," Stan sighed. "Most of the bus were on their way back from senior's day at the local mall. I let them off in front of the adult living building on fourth. Now that I think about it, I doubt many of them heard a word of what was happening." He gulped back a swig of beer, adding a huff after he swallowed.

"Was there anyone else?" Jeff asked, feeling the case slipping through his fingers.

"Hm," Stan hummed, scratching an eyebrow. The front legs of his chair crashed back down. "Actually, there was. Truly asked me what the lady was complaining about."

"Truly!" Jeff exclaimed.

"Yes," Stan continued, "she was riding that bus to work at the buffet."

"How do you know that's her name?" Jeff asked.

"She rides my usual route a lot," Stan replied. "We've talked before."

"Do you mind me asking where she normally goes?" Jeff inquired, his eyebrows arched in anticipation.

"What for?" Stan asked.

"She wasn't at the restaurant when we interviewed the staff," Jeff stated. "I'd like to track her down for a statement. She might have seen something that could help your case."

"I doubt that," Stan said, taking another swig of beer. "But I usually drop her outside the coffee shop she works at downtown."

"I thought she only worked there on weekends," Jeff commented.

"It's the closet stop to her other job a few blocks up the street. The only other place I have seen her go on a regular basis is a medical building. She sees a doctor there. Stevenson, I think she said his name was."

"Thank you for your time. I can see myself out." Jeff snapped closed his notebook. A new lead brought a smile to his face.

Chapter Seventeen

Jeff stood in the lobby, glancing over the list of white names stuck on a blackboard. Doctor Stevenson's office was on the second level. He glanced between the door to the stairs and the lift.

Doing the right thing for his health meant taking the extra steps. The up button turned orange while he continued his self-debate on the advantages and disadvantages of making the climb. The stairs never had a chance. He knew the whole time that the elevator would win. The option of being healthier would still exist come the next day.

The compartment shifted under his feet as he entered, each step rewarding him with an unnerving creak. His eyes darted to the posted use restrictions as the doors closed. There was no rhyme or reason as to why. He was only a few pounds over his goal weight and elevators were made to hold multiple people at the same time. The ride came to an abrupt stop, the lift jerking. He braced himself using the silver handrail. A snail moved quicker than the doors did opening. The stairs had made it back on the plan for today's activities. There was nothing that could make him ride in that ancient relic again.

The second floor was a plain hallway of shut doors that snaked left then right before ending at Doctor Stevenson's personal offices. He sucked in his breath, fully expecting a fight. Showing up at any medical professional's office without a warrant rarely went well. In fact, he could think of a single instance when it had panned out for him in the past. Still, here he was, bright-eyed and bushy-tailed, looking for a doctor to toss him a bone.

He marched in, freezing when he realized there wasn't a secretary to head him off at the pass. He glanced around the room, lost in confusion. If there was no ruckus, the good doctor wouldn't know he was busting in. He glanced at his knuckles. Shrugging his shoulders, he rapped on the door.

"Come in," Doctor Stevenson said.

Jeff poked his head inside the door. "Doctor Stevenson?" he asked.

"You can come in," the doctor snickered. "I don't bite."

"That's good to know," Jeff replied, flashing his badge. "I need to ask you a few questions about one of your clients."

Doctor Stevenson sighed. "Unless you have a warrant to go along with the badge, I'm afraid I can't help you. There are strict rules about patient confidentiality."

"I realize that," Jeff stated. "I was hoping you could shed some light on an ongoing investigation."

"I'm afraid I can't," Dr. Stevenson stated. "Out of curiosity, which client is it you are interested in?"

"Truly Alaney," Jeff replied.

"Truly," the doctor echoed, sitting forward. "She's a test subject for some data I'm gathering. I'm in the middle of writing a book with another doctor."

"Writing a book," Jeff said, taking a seat. The good doctor had provided an opening and he was going to take every inch he'd been given. "That's ambitious. It's hard to sell any books nowadays. Hitting a bestseller's list can make careers."

"Yes," the doctor agreed. "I do realize that. Everyone needs a niche. Ours is based on a hypnosis study. It's fascinating, but probably won't be made into a movie."

"You never know. Imagine the attention a book like yours would receive if it contained a case that helped the police department solve several murders," Jeff suggested.

"Murders," Doctor Stevenson repeated. "You believe Truly killed someone?"

Jeff shrugged his shoulders. "I can't be sure at this point. It's an ongoing investigation and releasing details to anyone outside of those actively involved in the case is against my oaths."

"But if we collaborated..."

"That would be a different story," Jeff stated. "You'd be an official adviser on the case and, after it is solved, could write about your involvement in your book. The press would be eating out of your hands. It has television series written all over it."

The doctor leaned back in his chair, lips held closed. "She signed a release for the study, so I have no professional obligations not to speak with you. Alright! I'll work with you. If there is a murder to be solved, I owe it to society."

"What can you tell me about Truly?" Jeff asked, pulling out his notebook and pencil.

"She has no memories of her childhood," the doctor explained. "No normal forms of therapy were working to help her regain them. That's when she agreed to the study."

"At what age did she lose her memories?" Jeff asked.

"It was fifteen years ago. She would have been nine," the doctor replied. "What happened in her past?"

"There were three accidents," Jeff explained. "A classmate, a man named Edgar who dated her mother, and her mother. All of them died within a week of each other."

"She mentioned her mother and Edgar in today's hypnosis session," the doctor stated. "There was mention of another man who she thought was responsible."

"Did she say who this man was?"

"It was a rather odd name, Damionion," the doctor replied.

"Onion?" Jeff scoffed. "Could she have been lying?"

"Doubtful," the doctor answered. "She was under the whole time. She actually believes every word she said. I didn't stay for the whole session as I had another patient to attend to. I was going to go over the footage today."

"Was there any mention of either Earl or Bernard?" Jeff asked. "They died in a similar fashion to the other three."

"Not while I was present," the doctor answered. "Was there anything unusual that ties the deaths together?"

"This might sound odd, but fortunes," Jeff admitted.

"That doesn't sound odd in the least." A grin smothered his lips. "It sounds fascinating." He held up a finger. "Let me explain. In today's session, Truly said that if she gave someone a fortune, Damionion made it come true."

"I was hoping to make that connection," Jeff said, a fire lit in his eyes.

"What other dots can I help connect?" the doctor asked, matching the detective's enthusiasm.

"Did she mention texting anyone? Someone sent a message to both victims just prior to their deaths using a non-traceable throwaway phone," Jeff explained.

"I can't say that she was the one texting," the doctor admitted. "But... Truly did mention that she forgot to pay her bill and her regular phone had been shut off. She was using a temporary one for a few days until the issues were resolved."

"That could be the phone we are looking for!" Jeff exclaimed. "This has been most helpful." He accepted one of the doctor's business cards, holding out one of his own in exchange. "I'll email you the important notes from the files. I'd like you to compare my notes with the results of your session. In the meantime, I still have a few other interviews to conduct."

"I'll review the footage and let you know if I find anything else that might help," the doctor offered, watching the detective's thumbs move with purpose over his phone's keyboard.

"That would be perfect," Jeff said without looking up. "I'd like to solve this puzzle before any more accidents happen."

"I'll do whatever I can to assist."

126

Jeff dialed his partner on the way out. "Hey. Where are you right now?"

"I left you a message," Miranda complained. "Didn't you listen to it?"

"I hate automated crap... you know that," Jeff replied. "I have good news. We have everything we need for the captain. I'd like to interview the officer before we do anything else."

"And I was on my way to see a psychic," Miranda said, chuckling.

"You might want to hear what I found out first," Jeff suggested. "Fortune telling is truly dangerous."

"Please tell me that wasn't a pun," Miranda pleaded. "I'll head back now. After we are done, I'm still going to see the psychic, though. I have a gut feeling there is something there we need to know."

"Trust the gut," Jeff said. "See you in a few."

Chapter Eighteen

"Here it is, Captain," Jeff said, tossing down a new set of files. "There are motives and connections all over this case."

"And my top detectives still can't knock before entering," the captain complained. "Head to interrogation room four. I'll send for Officer Doogalen and meet you there. Take these files off my desk, too."

"You haven't read them," Miranda commented.

"I trust you two aren't stupid enough to bother me without doing the required legwork!" the captain bellowed. "Now move before I change my mind."

Jeff grabbed his partner's arm and pulled her out of the office. "We have one chance at this, let's not blow it," he suggested. "We can plead our case in any room."

Miranda nodded. A swipe of her identification and the lock buzzed, a green light indicating they could proceed. The room was more of a sterilized cubicle than what one might expect from a place used for criminal interrogations.

Standard florescent tubes, hidden in the ceiling and covered by the same plastic as the captain's door, created a white glow, accentuating the lack of colour on the walls and flooring. The single perfectly-centred table was bolted to the ground. The surrounding plastic chairs reflected off its shiny metal surface.

The door shut behind them, locking. Miranda shivered, feeling the burdens of being on the opposite side of the law. The coin had flipped and, while she wasn't under investigation, their case was. Making a suspect wait was a tactic she'd employed on many an occasion. Anyone with even an inkling of doubt in their mind cracked under the pressure.

Miranda took a seat, the beginnings of tiny beads forming on her brow. The phrase *make them sweat it out* held new meaning for her. She'd never fully understood it before.

Jeff's hand on her shoulder took her by surprise. Her heart skipped a beat before rushing into overdrive.

"Relax," Jeff said. "Everything will be fine." He took a seat beside his partner.

Miranda flashed a meek smile. She had been in front of reporters, judges and committees throughout her career. Never once had any of those experiences frightened her as much as sitting there did. It wasn't logical. There was nothing at stake, other than her reputation. Of course, there was a foreboding sense looming in the back of her mind. If it was correct, her life was about to take a drastic turn and it was one she would never be able to come back from.

The buzz of the lock captured both their attentions before the door opened. It was time.

"Henry," Captain Miller announced, "I'd like you to meet two of my finest detectives, Jeff and Miranda."

"Pleasure," Jeff said, standing to offer his hand, while giving the man his standard once-over. He'd learnt long ago that the difference between walking the beat and investigating was being able to take notice of every detail, especially when it came to people. Years of being a detective had solidified that in his mind. It was second nature to him now.

Henry Doogalen wasn't a stereotypical officer. There was no uniform; instead he dressed in street clothes. He unzipped his windbreaker jacket, hanging it off the back of a chair. The signs of years of dedication to the force were etched into his face. They didn't take the form of normal scars, but every wrinkle had its own story behind it.

"Pleasure," he said, accepting Jeff's hand in a firm shake across the table. Placing his gray flat cap down, he took a seat. "What can I do for you youngins?" He chuckled.

Jeff's curiosity piqued, his inner investigator taking over. The man was clearly older than himself, but by how much? His once ginger hair held numerous lines of grey, matching his bushy moustache. That alone wasn't an indicator of age, though. It was more a testament to the man's strength in overcoming adversities. The signs were there that he'd faced and bested more than his fair share of those.

It was Henry Doogalen's physique that gave him away. It wasn't a case of him being in bad shape, but rather hitting that point in a man's life when age simply caught up. No amount of lifting or exercise stopped the effects of time. Taking that into account, the officer sitting across the table had to be a senior citizen.

"We'd like to ask you a few questions about some accidents that took place fifteen years ago," Jeff said.

"Fifteen years ago?" Henry chuckled, shifting in his seat. "Accidents aren't the most memorable cases."

"I think you'll remember these," Jeff suggested. "They all connected to a young girl named Truly."

Henry's head tilted back, his eyes meeting the lights above. "Truly DeCanter. I wondered if I'd ever hear that name again."

"So you do remember her!" Miranda exclaimed.

"Oh, yes," Henry admitted. "She'd be hard to forget. What is it you are looking for?"

"We believe she's living here in Knollville," Jeff replied. "Similar accidents to the ones fifteen years ago have started."

Henry brushed his hand over his moustache and lips. "An accident is an accident."

"Except when it's murder," Jeff argued. "Can you tell us what you know?"

Henry sighed. "I met Truly when I was first on the scene at a fire. Imagine finding a tiny girl in the middle of the night watching everything she knew burn up before her eyes. She stood barefoot on what little lawn there was, her faded pink nightgown blowing about her legs. She was a sight. The only things she had with her were a paper-thin plastic fish clenched tightly in one fist and her own hair in the other. Someone had chopped off her long braid. It still had a blue ribbon tied around it..."

"Edgar died in the fire, didn't he?" Jeff questioned.

The lines between Henry's brows deepened as he nodded, eyes glossed over. "Yes, Edgar was the sole victim of the fire, unless you count the house. The investigation showed he'd had a few too many and passed out while smoking. The cigarette fell into a glass of alcohol, creating a mini explosion."

"There was nothing suspicious about it at all?" Jeff questioned. "A fortune being left as a calling card."

Henry's gaze darted to his younger counterpart. "A fortune," he echoed. "Is that your connection between the deaths?" He pursed his lips together. "There was an ace of spades melted onto what was left of his forehead."

"The death card," Miranda gasped, her fingers covering her lips. "How did you explain that?"

"We didn't at the time," Henry admitted. "Truly claimed there was another man present that night. We invested all our resources into trying to find him."

"Did you?" Jeff questioned.

"No," Henry stated. "There was nothing to prove anyone else was there."

"Could Truly have been responsible for the fire?" Jeff scooted to the edge of his chair, hands clasped on the table.

"Could? That's an interesting term," Henry replied. "Almost anything is possible. The evidence suggested she didn't, though. Even if a nine-year-old could concoct such an elaborate plan, she most certainly couldn't carry it out alone. For her to place the cigarette in the alcohol, put her in danger's way. There would have been burns."

"Was she examined?" Miranda asked.

"Of course," Henry replied. "She had a thorough investigation and there were no recent burn marks."

"You said recent..."

"There were some signs that could have been taken as possible abuse," Henry blurted out. "Marks and scars were all over the girl. X-rays showed an array of fractured bones that had healed without medical help. We couldn't prove any of it, though. Before you ask... there were no signs of anything sexual. At that point, however, even if we found any conclusive evidence against the girl, no judge or jury would have convicted."

"So you dropped it," Jeff stated.

"There was nothing to drop," Henry argued. "As far as we were concerned, she was a victim herself."

"What about her mother, Geena?" Jeff asked.

Henry chuckled. "You have done your homework. Geena was another piece of work. She showed up at the department cussing. The officer on desk was a rookie. She was the biological mother and he took her in to see her daughter before informing me. I got there in time to stop the woman from slapping Truly across the face. Geena was higher than a kite and drunker than a skunk."

"How'd she die?" Miranda asked.

"Nobody knows for sure," Henry admitted. "We threw her into the drunk tank to sober her up. The room was sealed... no way out and no way in. There were regular rounds checking on her. Still, the next morning we found her dead. She appeared to have choked on her own vomit."

"So another accident," Jeff said, biting his bottom lip as he scribbled in his notebook. "Where did the fortune fit in?"

"It turned out the paper-thin plastic fish silhouette that Truly had been found with was used to tell fortunes. When placed in a person's hand, it curled up in different ways. The white sleeve it came in had a list of what the different actions meant."

"It worked like a mood ring," Miranda suggested.

"Exactly," Henry agreed. "We let her keep it since it was the only thing she saved from the house. Either her mother took it from her or Truly gave it to Geena in their brief meeting. At the autopsy, it was found stuck in her throat. That's what she choked on."

"Does a novelty item like that list bad fortunes?" Jeff asked. "I'd think it would be a fun item."

"If the fish is motionless, the corresponding fortune is listed as *dead one*," Henry said. "Draw your own conclusions."

"What happened to Truly?" Miranda questioned.

"The news of her mother's death was too much for her, she shut down for days. When she snapped out of it, her memories were gone. If you ask me, that was the first blessing the poor girl received in her entire life."

"Did you keep track of her?" Jeff asked.

"Child welfare came in," Henry replied. "A judge sealed her file. Truly was given a new life. I had no reason to interfere. The universe corrects things on its own sometimes. When it does, we should let it. Besides, she couldn't have been responsible for her mother's death. Geena and Truly were both alone at the time. That we can prove."

"What about the fortunes?" Jeff asked. "Are you saying they were a mere coincidence? And the school girl, Priscilla?"

"If there is one thing in life I've learnt, it's that there are no coincidences." Henry sighed. "I don't believe Truly committed any murders. Was she involved in some way? Possibly, but probably not consciously. All three deceased individuals had hurt her. A fortune appeared to have been given to each by her as well. That, however, in my opinion, is as far as her role went. What happened after, we may never fully understand."

"People are dying!" Jeff exclaimed. His chair scraped against the floor as he stood. "It's our job to figure it out and stop it."

Henry turned his attention to Captain Miller. "They have a lot to learn," he said.

"They'll get there," the captain replied. His phone vibrated on the table. "Miller here." He paused. "Okay, thanks." The phone disappeared into his shirt pocket. "Did you get everything you needed?"

"Yeah," Jeff huffed.

"Good, cause there is someone here to see you."

Chapter Nineteen

Truly flopped back on her couch, allowing herself to sink into the softness. She shut her eyes, trying to remember something, anything from her session with Doctor Sven. She had been there for a couple of hours and that time was as blank as her childhood. These sessions were supposed to help her remember, not steal more memories away.

Only you can decide to open your mind.

She covered her face with a throw pillow. Hearing voices didn't make her feel any more sane. Her own insecurities almost drowned out the light knocking. Her door swung open before she had a chance to answer.

"Hey," Maria said. "I've been trying to get in touch with you. Where you been?"

"Going crazy," Truly snorted. "Wanna come?"

"I'll pass, thanks." She plopped down on the opposite side of the couch. "Did the police come and talk to you?"

"Police?!" Truly shrieked. "Why would the police want to talk to me?"

"You haven't heard?!" Maria gasped. "The accident the other day up the street from the coffee shop... that was Earl. He's dead. They found one of our coffee cups and the horoscope page. It was an accident, but they said they still had to look into it."

"Wow," Truly said. "I can't believe he's actually dead."

"Yeah," Maria agreed. "Talk about karma, huh. What are the odds he'd pull a crap move on you then get squished by a truck right after?"

"Way to make me feel better," Truly complained.

"At least he can't harass any other women," Maria said. "No one deserves to be treated like that..."

"Is that the reason for the visit?" Truly questioned. "Cause if it is, I'm sorry, but death doesn't become me today."

Maria chuckled. "Actually," she said, her hands moving along with her lips. "I came to share some exciting news. We won't have to wear stupid uniforms or work multiple jobs much longer." Her bottom bounced on the couch.

"Why not?" Truly asked, skeptical.

"Because," Maria started with a toothy grin, "a new plant is opening its headquarters right here in Knollville."

"A plant?!" Truly's nose scrunched up. "What type of plant?"

"The best type... makeup." Maria swooned. "They are already looking for all sorts of positions from development to sales. I'm going to pick up applications. You wanna come?" She waggled her eyebrows.

"I'm burnt out," Truly replied. "If I don't catch a few winks, I might not make it to tomorrow."

"No problem," Maria said. "I'll grab you one of each application. After you sleep, we'll fill them in together. Deal?"

"Deal." Truly alternated glances between her friend and the door. Someone else was knocking. "Grand central station..." she mumbled, turning the handle.

"Hi," a man said. "I know you. You were my server from the other night?"

"At the buffet," Truly agreed, nodding. "I remember. You didn't track me down for an order of egg rolls, did you?"

"No," he replied. "I'm here to replace your appliances. I need the measurements to make sure they fit correctly."

"I thought I wasn't getting any new appliances," Truly scoffed. "Or anything else around here fixed." She returned to the couch, leaving the door open.

"We'll get it all fixed up for you," the man offered. "Things are going to change around here."

"Don't tell me Mr. Bailey had a change of heart," Truly snickered.

"You don't know?" the man said. "I assumed because you were our waitress you were there..."

"The words *you don't know* are starting to make me feel sick today," Truly blurted out. "Your table stayed after my shift had ended. The owners let me go immediately after the bill was paid."

"There was an accident," the man said. "Bernard Bailey was run over by a bus."

"What?!" Truly gasped. "I had no idea."

"The weird thing is his fortune warned him," the man said, shaking his head. "I've never seen a cookie predict death before."

"A fortune," Truly whispered, one hand covering her mouth. She fell back onto the couch.

"Looks like karma is really kicking some butt for you this week," Maria mumbled. "I'm going to grab those applications."

Truly didn't notice anyone leave, but simply found herself alone with her own thoughts.

Fortunes.

She reached for her purse, pulling out the package Maria had bought for her. Each remaining item stared back at her from where she laid them out on her coffee table. Taking stock of her fortune telling collection, she blinked several times before grabbing the plastic sleeve holding the fun fish. It crinkled into a ball in her fist, preparing to go for a dip. She flushed the toilet, doubting it knew how to swim.

In the end, there were only two items she convinced herself to keep: the pen, because she was always looking for one, and a token coin for good luck. She tossed both back into her purse. If people's deaths were being foretold, she had another reason to hate fortunes.

Another knock on the door caught her by surprise. "Doctor Stevenson," she said. "What are you doing here?"

"I need you to come with me," the doctor replied. "It's a matter of life and death."

Chapter Twenty

"What do you think?" Jeff asked.

"About these two?" Captain Miller huffed, turning up the volume on the monitor. "She's the girl?"

"Yeah," Jeff admitted, rubbing his neck. He had expected to hear from Doctor Stevenson again, but not for him to show up at the department with his suspect.

"What, did he do a citizen's arrest?" Captain Miller shook his head. "I hope this mess doesn't blow up in your face. You better get in there."

Jeff nodded, knowing he needed to be in the room with them. If Truly did happen to confess, only an officer could accept it.

"Doctor Stevenson." Jeff said, extending his hand for a firm shake. He wasn't about to let someone roll in and take control of his investigation.

"What's going on? I thought this was a matter of life and death," Truly complained, pacing like a caged animal.

"That it is," Doctor Stevenson replied, motioning for her to join him at the table.

Jeff took a stance in a corner of the room, deciding to allow the doctor his theatrics.

"I know what you've done," the doctor said. "I've been going over police files and my own for hours. I know about the murders and I know how you pulled them off."

"Murders?!" Truly shrieked. "I haven't done anything and I resent the accusations."

"Oh, you did," the doctor continued. "I believe Bernard Bailey was the intended target the whole time. Earl was a dry-run, so to speak, opportunity presenting itself at the time."

"Really?!" she snorted. "Why?"

"It was no secret that you had issues with your landlord over rent and repairs," the doctor explained. "It was his proposal that you work off what you couldn't afford that threw you over the edge... in a similar way to what happened fifteen years ago."

"I don't remember what happened fifteen years ago," Truly argued, crossing her arms over her chest.

"Oh, I think you do," the doctor stated. "Your plan was good. It took quite a bit for me to connect the dots. The phone was the first thing. You let your payment date pass on purpose, allowing you to obtain a limited use and non-traceable one for the week without arising suspicion."

"I forgot to pay my bill," Truly snarled. "Lots of people don't make payments on time."

"You were still formulating a plan for your landlord when Earl gave you what you needed to try things out. You took his table without argument, knowing he would harass any waitress. He always did."

"It was my turn to serve him," Truly answered.

"It was a slow morning, as usual," the doctor continued, ignoring her. "You'd read the newspaper already, leaving it open at the horoscopes."

"Maria found the horoscope. She showed it to me. You can ask her," Truly protested.

"Yes," the doctor agreed. "She found it because you left it for her to find. Then you circled it in red and handed it to Earl. While your coworkers were amused with him reading the prediction, you took the opportunity to unzip your uniform a smidgen more."

"Don't be ridiculous," Truly complained.

"You knew Earl was a dirty old man. That mixed with a touch of anger and he couldn't help but take your bait." The doctor stood, placing both his hands on a chair and leaning forward. "Tell me, why you didn't complain when he groped you?"

"He took me by surprise," Truly replied. "I froze."

The doctor wagged a finger at her. "That's what you wanted people to think. No, you were giving him a powerful drug... hope. After you let him feel a bit, he believed he had a chance with you."

"What?!" Truly shrieked. "You're insane."

The doctor laughed. "Playing the victim gave you the freedom to sit in the corner without attention. Human nature kept Al and Maria from looking in your direction. No one wants to feel pity. That was your chance. You had Earl's number, he'd just given it to you with the tip. You used the pay-as-you-go phone to text him some naughty things."

"How could I have known he was going to step off a curb into traffic at that moment?" Truly argued.

"Because you've walked it," the doctor answered. "You work as a cashier at the store on the same corner Earl died. Working there, you must have seen Earl's path. Like you, he didn't drive. Also, the closest bus stop to the store is in front of the coffee shop. You would have known exactly how long it took to make the trek to that spot. Your timing didn't have to be exact, as long as you had his attention in the moments before he reached the intersection."

"How could I possibly know he wouldn't look up?" she argued.

"Your earlier meeting and the nature of the texts had Earl aroused," the doctor stated. "He wasn't thinking with his brain at the time. You counted on that."

"What happened to patient-doctor confidentiality?" Truly asked. "Why are you here?" Her eyes narrowed, scrutinizing the man.

"I'm here to put a stop to a serial killer," the doctor announced. "You did sign a release the other day."

Truly's fingers covered her lips. "The book," she huffed. "This is about money."

"I admit, helping in a police investigation is a bonus feature in my soon-to-be-released bestseller," the doctor stated. "But I have a moral obligation as well. Bernard was a bit trickier for you to pull off."

"How so?" Truly scoffed.

"The plan had to formulate on the fly. You only learned what time the bus would be racing by a few moments prior to your shift," the doctor explained. "And it wasn't until you reached the restaurant that you were informed about Mr. Bailey's reservation.

I'm guessing he asked for you as a server to reinforce his dominance over your position in life. He must have pulled you aside at some point, giving you an ultimatum."

"I served him dinner," Truly said. "Wouldn't it have been easier to poison him if I wanted him dead?"

"That would have been investigated," the doctor argued. "You wanted it to appear as an accident as the other cases fifteen years ago."

"Other cases?" she snapped. "What other cases?"

"I'll get to those," the doctor said. "One murder at a time. I do have to mention Edgar, though, as he was good enough to teach you sleight of hand. That was what allowed you to switch Bernard's cookie with one that contained a bad fortune. You left work as soon as the bill was paid and texted Mr. Bailey from outside, allowing him precisely the right amount of time to reach the street. My guess is you waited across the road for him, creating the distraction that led to his death. Then you hid in the bushes, sneaking away when a crowd gathered."

"I didn't do any of this!" Truly barked.

"I suppose Damionion did," the doctor said.

Truly darted a glance in his direction. "Damionion," she repeated.

"Yes," the doctor said. "The man a nine-year-old's mind made up. You wanted a father... someone to care for you... someone to protect you..."

"I didn't," she stuttered.

"Your mind couldn't handle the deeds you had done," the doctor continued. "This strange man was born just for that role."

"No!" Truly screamed. Tears falling down her face pooled on her reflection in the metal table.

"You heard your mother say he was a crooked man," the doctor continued, ignoring her pleas to stop. "She meant in a criminal manner. To a young girl, however, that word drew a picture of a warped spine and a long bent nose to match. You called him a magic man."

"Stop!" Truly covered her ears.

"He took care of anyone who hurt you," the doctor stated. "The bully at school... Geena's abusive boyfriend... the neglectful mother... none of them deserved to live. Isn't that right?"

"They were horrible," she snarled, her memories flooding back. She wiped a tear from her cheek.

A grin formed over the doctor's lips. "And more recently, Earl the groper and Bernard the harasser. Why don't you admit you killed them? We have enough evidence in my files and the hypnosis footage for a conviction."

I didn't," Truly stated. "I admit I gave them all fortunes, but that was the end of my role."

"If you knew what would happen," Jeff said from the corner, "that makes you, at the minimum, an accomplice to murder."

"I didn't," Truly squeaked. "I can't control fortunes or the future. I merely offered a vessel for a fortune to be told. Each person decided for themselves to look and what they said."

"And your memories?" the doctor questioned.

"Came back just now," Truly admitted. "I guess I should thank you for that. Your treatment was at least successful in that regard. You may want to rethink your bedside manner, though."

"Doctor Stevenson," Jeff said, motioning for him to step outside the room, "thank you for your help. With your testimony and files, I believe we have a solid case. I know you are itching to start work on the book."

The doctor shook his hand. "With any luck, I will have it ready for release on the heels of the hearing. If you need anything else, you know where to find me."

Jeff stepped back inside the room, two officers joining him. "Truly Alaney, you are under arrest in connection with the deaths..."

"If you really want to catch the one who killed these people," Truly blurted out, "there's a fortune telling pen in my purse. You simply click it and read the message on the side. I'm giving it to you. Use it, if you have the nerve. Just be aware. If you use it, he will come..."

Chapter Twenty-One

The fortune teller's parlour was one of several buildings in the downtown core that had lacked a tenant for quite a few years despite having ample parking and being located on a bus route. Without any operating businesses, the owner had left the property to collect dust. With boarded-up windows on one side and a for rent sign on the other, the occult store and museum looked right at home.

Miranda slammed her car door, wondering what she had gotten herself into. The smell of incense attacked her nostrils before the front door had a chance to open. Inside, jars containing sticks and cones of every fragrance lined the walls.

"Hello?" she called out. No one replied.

Miranda moved further inside, winding her way through displays of candles and holders. She chuckled at the section of novelty items located next to the cash register. Even psychics needed to make a living.

"Hello?" Miranda called out again. "Is anyone here?"

A beaded curtain rattled, moving aside to allow a woman to pass through. "I apologize," she offered, her words almost singing. "How can I help you?"

Miranda glanced at the woman's name tag. "Zulana," she said, flashing her badge. "I need to ask you a few questions."

"I knew you were coming," Zulana stated. "Come into the back. We can have a chat." She led the way, returning through the beads. "Have a seat. Now, what can I do for you?"

Miranda glanced around the room at the array of unusual artifacts and pictures. Her eyes settled on a wooden carving of a man bent over at the waist. "I wanted to ask you about various devices used in fortune telling."

"I have a feeling you aren't talking about crystal balls or runes," Zulana replied.

"No," Miranda agreed. "I have an interest in some of the items that are produced as novelties. Could they be used to give an accurate reading of future events?"

The woman puckered her lips, twitching them from side to side. "The thing most people don't realize about psychics is that items through which the reading is conducted are not where power is held. A simple flame can be used to bring forth visions. They are merely tools of the trade."

"So it is possible to use a paper fortune telling game to predict the future?" Miranda asked.

"Quite," Zulana answered. "Although a seasoned psychic isn't likely to pick that as a conduit to manifest a vision from."

Miranda's eyes returned to the sculpture. "You have quite a collection. I understand there is a museum here as well. Is there a history attached to fortune telling?"

Zulana cackled. "Everything has a history," she replied, picking up the figurine. "It is deities I think you would like to know more about."

"Deities?" Miranda echoed. "There are fortune telling gods?"

"There are," she answered, holding up a bundle of sage. "Do you mind?"

Miranda shook her head, watching the woman as she lit the dried bundled leaves.

"That's better," Zulana said. "Where was I... oh, yes. There are two sides to every deity. Think of the world we live in as a large mirror. On one side, we have a divine master of fortunes."

"His reflection would be the opposite?" Miranda questioned, trying to follow the logic.

"Yes, a divine master of misfortune, if you will," Zulana explained. "That's what keeps this world in balance. Neither one can outdo the other. They are one and the same, yet opposite."

"Can they manifest in our world?" Miranda asked.

Frown lines appeared on Zulana's face. "There are some times, when the stars align correctly, when that can happen. Most deities, however, have little interest in the mortal world. For lack of a better explanation, we bore them."

"Are there any reasons why they might show interest in someone here?"

Zulana howled a laugh. "From time to time, they have been known to take interest in mortal mating."

Miranda sighed. "Any other reason?"

"If a previous trip here produced a child," Zulana replied. "They would take an interest in their own offspring's life. It would be difficult, though. Even supreme deities need a door to be unlocked. There has to be a connection... a way in and out of this world."

"What about devices used for fortune telling?" Miranda questioned.

Zulana's eyes shifted from side to side. "That's a good question. It would have to be someone with power operating the device."

"An offspring," Miranda suggested.

"Yes, that would do it," Zulana agreed. "This is a specific situation, though. The odds are astronomically against it ever happening."

Miranda glanced at the wooden statue again. "Is that the divine master of misfortune?"

"I've never met him personally," Zulana admitted, chuckling. "But I have been told it is an exact likeness."

"Hypothetically speaking," Miranda started, "if there was such a child and said child was hurt by someone, could a bad fortune be brought to pass?"

Zulana's tongue peeked out the corner of her mouth. "Huh," she grunted. "Let's put it this way, I wouldn't want to be the one on the receiving end of a fortune from that child."

"So the device being used would be a connection strong enough to allow a deity to visit for a short time?" Miranda questioned.

"Undoubtedly," Zulana said. "The police department would also have a few unexplained deaths on their hands. If this is happening, beware. Your involvement could be construed as harmful to the child in question. You may want to stay clear of any form of fortune telling, novelty or otherwise."

"Thank you," Miranda said, standing. "You've been most helpful."

"I am always happy to aid those in need," Zulana stated. "Most who carry a badge are not willing to accept the advice I give, though. I am glad you came to me."

"I hope we can meet again someday," Miranda said. "Under better circumstances."

"We will," Zulana replied.

Miranda had one hand on her phone before a foot was out the door. "Pick up, Jeff," she said, starting her car. She sighed at the sound of his voicemail message. "Jeff, I am on my way back. Do me a favour, don't touch anything that could predict the future until after we talk."

Chapter Twenty-Two

Doctor Stevenson leaned back in his chair, allowing it to spin around in the circle. It wasn't often he indulged in celebrations, but today was special. Originally, his book plans had involved self-publishing. After aiding in a live police investigation, however, he had already secured a full book deal, and along with it a sizable advance. All it took was a single phone call. Who said crime didn't pay? Maybe not for the criminals, but it sure did for him.

A USB stick twirled between his fingers, his own personal baton. His lips curled up as he inserted it into his laptop to watch the footage of the hypnosis session once again.

"Poor girl," he snickered. "The only one foolish enough to sign the release without a lawyer. Maybe if you'd had a father to protect you, things would have been different all around. It really is truly unfortunate." He laughed at his own joke.

He was a man with no conscience. In his profession, that was how it had to be. Still, Truly's voice nagged at the back of his mind, daring him to test his theory.

He slid open his desk drawer, his hand fetching a bottle of bourbon to celebrate his soon-to-be success. The cap twisted, snapping its safety seal. The golden brown liquid flowed evenly into a cup.

"Damn!" he cussed, wiping spilled alcohol from his suit. The bottle landed firmly on his desk, his gaze fully captivated by another item lurking in the drawer; the still-closed gift Truly had presented to him.

His fingers tingled, shying away from opening the packaging. He chuckled, renewing his faith in his own abilities as a psychiatrist. No one mocked his intelligence and got away with it. The flimsy plastic seal had no chance when faced with the sharp edge of his letter opener.

"A fake, through and through," he mumbled, chuckling. Taking the sphere in his hand, he tossed it in the air. Its contents swirled, clouding its once-clear surface. "Let's see what my future has in store." His fist clamped around it on the way back down.

Opening his fingers slowly, the murky cloud began to dissipate. Black letters began to form. He gasped as they formed a word... *DEATH.*

"Nice touch," he snickered, "but I have you figured out." He slammed the ball down on his desk. His laptop sputtered, the screen turning black.

"Stupid battery! At least now, I can afford to buy a new computer and I owe it all to Truly."

He'd never admit to being on the verge of bankruptcy, but truth be told, his finances as of late hadn't been stellar. The book deal was the break he needed to stay afloat. If it weren't for Truly coming along, he would have been out on his ass in another three months.

Grabbing his cord, he plugged the computer in, hoping to juice it up one more time. Sparks flew. A shock knocked him backwards into a sitting position. The wheels on his chair took over, spinning in circles, the force of his landing fuelling their movement across the perfectly polished floors. His feet tried to stop the motion, tangling in the mix. As he fell, the last thing he saw was flames erupting on his desk, inching closer to the bottle of bourbon. He would die exactly as Edgar did fifteen years ago and Truly was nowhere to be found. He'd been wrong, all along.

A crooked shadow fell over him. "You!" The world went dark. The doctor's last breath was taken knowing he'd been bested by a nine-year-old girl.

Chapter Twenty- Three

"Jeff," Captain Miller said, sticking his head in the detective's office, "I thought you should know, a team just returned from a fire scene. Doctor Stevenson was inside the building at the time. He didn't make it." He sighed.

"He's dead..."

"You won't like this," the captain said, rubbing the back of his neck. "Initial reports classify it as an accident. A bad laptop battery seems to be the culprit. I thought you'd want to see this." He held up a plastic bag containing the fortune telling sphere. "It was found at the scene."

"Shouldn't it be in evidence?" Jeff questioned, placing his phone face-down in front of him.

"I'll let you decide that," the captain answered. "I've put all the files and evidence in interrogation room four. You can look through it if you want."

"Doctor Stevenson's records..."

"Were destroyed." Captain Miller pursed his lips together. "The data from the hypnosis session, too. I don't need to tell you..."

It was Jeff's turn to finish his captain's words. "There is no case without Stevenson."

"Yeah," the captain said.

"Have you turned her loose yet?" Jeff asked.

The captain let out an audible huff. "I wanted to tell you first. I'm on my way down to holding to sign the release papers."

Jeff bit his bottom lip, nodding. "Mind if I add that to the case file?" he asked, motioning to the evidence bag.

"Be my guest," the captain replied, handing the sphere to him. "I'd like to talk to you when Miranda returns. Stick around in room four for me."

The walk down the corridor was the longest of his career. The bitter taste of failure had control of his taste buds. He bit his tongue, drawing blood in the hopes that the coppery taste would outweigh that of his own inadequacies.

The green light flashed, followed by the low buzz of the door lock complying with his request to enter. His eyes fixated on the two white banker boxes that had been placed on the metal table; one from fifteen years ago and the other the recent cases. Sitting there alone, they stuck out worse than a blemish on a super model.

He lifted the lid on the more recent of the two, tossing the plastic wrapped sphere inside. The corner of his eye caught a glimpse of a white and black pen. His hand shook, removing it. That innocent pen held all the answers he craved. How badly did he want to know the truth?

Chapter Twenty-Four

Miranda rushed down the hall, a sense of urgency pulsing through her veins. She'd never been a true believer, but this case had her second-guessing the boundaries of reality. A part of her couldn't help but hope her partner received her call and hadn't done anything stupid. The odds were against her; Jeff never listened to his voicemail messages.

She hopped from foot to foot, waiting for the red light to turn green. Grasping the handle too soon, the lock refused to open. She started the process all over again, jumping around worse than a child in need of a bathroom. This time, she waited for the buzz followed by the lock grinding open before she pulled.

Her first sight was her partner sitting at the sterile table. A black and white pen rolled back and forth between his hands. His gaze never once faltered from its movements.

"Jeff," Miranda said, her voice squeaking. She cleared her throat with a hoarse cough. "Please tell me you didn't use that thing."

Jeff chuckled. "I don't need to write anything," he said, pushing the pen towards the middle of the table. He slouched back in the plastic chair.

"That's not what I meant," Miranda snapped.

"I know what you meant," Jeff answered, frowning. "In the end, I didn't have the nerve."

"Good," Miranda said, taking a seat across from her partner. "It might sound crazy, but after talking to the psychic, I think there might be more to Damionion than we might want to admit."

Jeff let out a huff. "Ya think?" he replied. "Doctor Stevenson is dead. It was an accident, of course. A fire took not only his life, but his life's work, too. A novelty fortune-telling ball survived. It was found rolling around the ashes. It's in the box."

"Truly?"

"Gone," Jeff said, sitting up. "The captain released her when all the evidence went up in smoke."

"Where does that leave us?" Miranda asked.

"With two boxes to carry to storage," Captain Miller replied from the door. "I'll walk with you." He motioned with his head for the detectives to follow. They caught up to him waiting for their ride down to arrive.

Whoever created the elevator didn't have comfort in mind. The tiny cubicle boasted a certificate stating over a dozen people could ride at once. After piling the three of them and two boxes in, they were no more than sardines jammed into a can. No one said it, but with little room to move, they were all secretly thanking their lucky stars their companions all showered and wore deodorant on a daily basis.

Jeff detached his security pass to swipe access to the files room.

"I got it," the captain said, removing a card from his pocket. He turned his back to the doors.

The lift's gears began to grind, halting the descent, but the doors remained closed.

"Other way," the captain whispered.

Jeff and Miranda exchanged glances before turning to face the back of the elevator. It opened to a dimly-lit corridor they had never seen before.

"I thought we were going to file these," Miranda stated. "The Knollville case files are kept in a room the other way."

"Yes," Captain Miller agreed, "but the Knollville curse files are kept through there."

"Knollville curses?!" Miranda shrieked, quickening her pace to catch up to her partner who was already leaps and bounds ahead.

A set of double doors, which belonged in a hospital rather than a police department, stood between Jeff and the understanding he needed. He pushed hard, sending them swinging open. Inside was a complete duplicate of the department above them, lacking only officers at each of the desks.

"You made it, I see!" Henry Doogalen declared. "I was wondering if the captain's intuition about you two was a bit off."

"Can I ask..." Jeff started.

"This department handles unexplained files," the captain stated. "Most of the cases that end up down here require a certain willingness to take a few leaps of faith on the part of the investigators, in order to be solved."

"Are we talking paranormal or alien?" Jeff asked.

"Both," Henry answered, a grin peeking out from under his moustache. "Have you ever noticed that Knollville isn't on any map?"

"Not really," Jeff replied, shrugging his shoulders. "Most people have a GPS nowadays."

"How ancient I've become," Henry chuckled. "Let me rephrase that... have you noticed if you leave Knollville and use your GPS to return, the woman calling out directions at you becomes a bit confused? She might tell you to take a U-turn a few hundred times on the same road or ask you to veer to the left, landing you in a lake."

"No," Jeff admitted. "If I leave here, I pretty much know how to get back. I don't use a GPS."

"Okay," Henry said. "If you did, you would have noticed. Knollville is the hardest place in existence to find when you don't know where it is."

"What does this have to do with anything?" Miranda asked. "We patrol what happens in Knollville."

"Because of its secluded nature, Knollville attracts some unusual individuals," Henry replied. "You can read up on some of the recent cases if you want. Bottom line, we live in a paranormal hotspot. This department polices that side of things."

"What does that have to do with us?" Jeff asked.

"Henry is retiring," the captain announced. "He's well past the age and is lacing up the boots. All we've been waiting for is the right duo to come along to fill them. I would like the two of you to take a hold of the reins."

"You want us to become ghost hunters?" Miranda questioned, her nose crinkling up.

Henry chuckled. "In a sense, yes," he replied. "It's a whole lot more, too. You witnessed yourself how normal residents can become tangled in the affairs of the supernatural. You two would be ensuring their safety."

"We couldn't save anyone this time," Jeff scoffed. "What makes you think we can serve and protect against a herd of zombies?"

"I've worked this department for fifteen years and I don't have that answer," Henry admitted. "I do know we, as officers, have a duty to do our best to keep good people safe. No one is asking any more than that."

"Fifteen years?" One of Jeff's eyebrows arched as he glanced at the older officer. "That was when..."

"When I met Truly," Henry replied. "Yes. That case has haunted me my whole career. I imagine it will do the same to you.

Even in this department, in most of the files, the loose ends tie together creating a satisfactory ending... a hard to believe one, but it's closure nonetheless. When it comes to Truly, we may never know if those deaths belonged in this department, were accidents or should have been treated as unsolved murders."

"So a part of you does believe the girl could have been to blame," Jeff stated.

"As I said before, *could have* is a broad term," Henry explained. "The thought was always there that Geena might have been the only accidental death. I'll always have questions. Was there a man? If yes, was he of a supernatural descent? If no, was Truly behind it all?" He sighed.

"Who else would we be working with?" Jeff questioned.

"You would report to me," the captain stated. "No one else needs to know about your work. You have the full resources of the department at your fingertips at all times. The positions come with a pay increase as well."

Miranda shrugged her shoulders. "I'm in," she blurted out. "When do we start?"

Jeff darted a glance in her direction.

"What?!" she asked. "I enjoyed checking out the psychic shop. There's a whole world out there you and I chose to ignore. I, for one, am opening my eyes." She snapped her fingers.

"I guess you have two new paranormal detectives," Jeff said, rubbing his hands together. "Where do we start?"

Chapter Twenty-Five

Truly collected her things. Her eyes widened, pulling her lips into a mischievous grin; the pen was gone. A simple click was all it took for judgement to be passed on the detective for dragging her through the most painful experiences of her life all over again.

Linking her purse on one arm, she headed out the rotating doors funnelling people in and out of the building. Her legs couldn't move fast enough, racing down the front steps to the sidewalk.

It was night, although she had no idea what day. Inside a cell, time held no meaning. She had simply existed. It was a life wasted, without purpose.

She glanced back at the police department with disgust. They could have at least provided her with a ride home. Instead, they opted to set her free to walk in the dark without giving any thought to her safety.

Looking before leaping, she made sure no vehicles were coming before crossing the road. If there was a lesson to be learnt from the past week, it was street safety came first.

The quickest route home led through the park. Even in the dark, the trickling of the fountain remained a constant, beckoning her to stop for a moment to enjoy freedom once again. She complied, letting her fingers dance across the surface of the cool water. Coins littered the bottom of the basin, glistening in the moonlight. Come dawn they'd be gone, harvested by Knollville. Politicians were always stealing people's wishes.

Her reflection pouted back at her. There wasn't any money in her wallet to make a wish with... there was, however, a coin. Her eyes lit up as her hand plunged into the depths of the unknown; her purse. Feeling around, she wondered for a moment if it would ever return. Her breath escaped along with clenched fingers securing the good luck coin Maria had bought her. She tossed it in the air, a smile replacing her previous pout. Just as she thought things were looking up, a voice called out from behind her.

"I'll take that," a man said.

She glanced over the shoulder of her own reflection into the depths of the eyes of a criminal.

She chuckled. This situation summed up her luck perfectly. With an empty wallet and footsteps from the police department, a man held a gun to her back. If it was her luck he wanted, he could have it. It wasn't much good anyways.

The coin lobbed in the air, forcing her mugger to dive. Still, he was able to catch it easily.

"Now the purse," he demanded, waving the gun in her direction. "Make it snappy."

"There isn't anything in it," she complained.

"I'll be the judge of that!" he argued, grabbing the strap. The clasp snapped, leaving way to sights inside. He rummaged through the receipts and candy wrappers, coming up empty. "Great, I pick the poorest broad in Knollville." He shoved her purse back into her chest. "But I still got this. I think I'll let it decide your fate."

She stumbled backwards, falling. Pain radiated through her head and back. Her hand felt for a lump, returning wet with her own blood. She blinked several times, trying to remain focused.

The mugger tossed her lucky coin in the air. Catching it on the way back down, he flipped it over on the back of his hand. "It is truly unfortunate that both sides are the same." He chuckled.

"You are right about two things. Truly is my name," she replied, a glimmer of sass reflecting in her eyes. She stood without so much as a wobble, the fall a distant memory.

"And?" The man glanced down at the coin, his smile disappearing. The prediction of a lucky future vanished before his eyes, replaced by blood gushing from the coin. He dropped it, jumping back a step.

"And bad fortunes are my father's game," she said, howling a laugh.

The man glanced into the water, seeing a third reflection. He spun around, but no one was there. His feet tangled. At first, he managed to stay upright, stumbling over a construction cone, his arms flailing in caution tape. One foot hit a patch of cement still drying from a recent pour. He twisted, falling face first into the wet concrete. The drying process sped up, encasing him in a statuesque form.

Truly walked over, allowing her foot to kick the only flesh part of him left exposed, his butt.

"Thanks, Dad," she said. "Can I go home with you now?"

A tall man, partially hunched over at the midsection, stepped out of the shadows. With a tip of his hat, he bowed, extending his arm for his daughter to take.

"You were always welcome with me, dear," he said. "Are you sure you want to leave all you know behind?"

"I never fit into this world anyways," Truly replied. "Knollville is a nice place to visit, but I'm done with living here."

His cane came down, hitting the ground twice. Trees grew a path before her eyes, the familiar checkerboard tile leading the way to her throne.

She felt a light breeze kiss her bare shoulders, her mundane clothes having transformed into the beautiful wine-coloured strapless dress from her hypnosis session. Similar to Damionion's unusual jacket, it flowed to the ground in the back; the front cut short exposing her legs and drawing attention to a pair of black high heels.

There was no need to glance back. Her future lay ahead of her now and she was in control of it. She was finally the princess she had always wanted to be.

Chapter Twenty-Six

Jeff shivered. Hospitals were the worst place for any officer to have to go. It wasn't only the lurking illnesses waiting to attach themselves to another victim and be freed from their confines. Those he could handle with hand sanitizer and a bit of common sense. There was something far worse, however, that loomed over large medical facilities - a bleakness that attached itself to anyone walking through the entrance.

The double doors slid open on cue when he approached, offering to accept him freely as long as he checked all hope before passing through. Everything from that point on was void of colour, from the grey of the walls to the white of the doctor's jackets. Even if they removed them, underneath would have been a dark suit with crisp white linen shirt.

The face of the nurse behind the intake desk of the emergency department reminded him it was only the beginning of the journey. The real gloom and doom was yet to come. He flashed his badge at the woman separated from the waiting area by a glass partition.

"Come through." Her monotone voice and expressionless glare cut at his heart strings as precisely as a surgeon with a scalpel. The longer he remained, the more he would lose, severing his attachment to all that made him human.

Her head bobbed towards a set of doors opening on her right. He followed the corridor to his partner already waiting.

"What happened?"

Miranda sighed. "It looks like a mugging gone wrong. I'll tell you one thing, this guy has balls. I know it was night, but attacking someone in a park across the street from an entire police department."

"Have you been in?" Jeff asked.

"Yeah," Miranda replied, a sigh escaping her lips at the end of the word. "I had a chance to speak to the doctor, too. With extensive brain damage, there is no chance of coming back from this."

Jeff shook his head, walking into the multi-bed ward. "You have a copy of the medical reports?"

"I do," Miranda replied, leading the way to a cubicle enclosed by a curtain divider. She pulled back one section, allowing enough room for them both to enter.

Jeff stood at the edge of the bed staring at the victim. His pursed lips opened enough to allow a huff of air to escape. "I guess Henry was right... karma does have a way of fixing things in the end. I suppose we have a satisfactory end to our unsolved cases, too."

"Yeah," Miranda agreed. "Somehow, it's not as good a feeling as I thought it would be."

"I don't know," Jeff disagreed. "She looks peaceful... happy, even. Do we know how it happened?"

"The doctors say she has bruising on her chest from being pushed. That caused her to fall. The back of her head caught the edge of the fountain. A little harder and she might have died. Instead, Knollville is going to have to foot some medical bills. She's in a coma from which she'll never wake up again," Miranda explained.

"Life in a dream can be better than reality," Jeff said. "Wherever she is, I have a feeling things are better for her. What about the mugger?"

Miranda grimaced. "Justice might have been served. It was dark and he stumbled into the construction zone. We found him face-down in a patch of concrete. Needless to say... deceased."

"Please tell me there wasn't anything lying around that predicted his demise," Jeff requested.

"Nope," Miranda answered. "All he had was a good luck coin."

"Well, it didn't work," Jeff commented. "He wasn't very lucky, was he?"

"No," Miranda agreed. "One might say he was truly unfortunate..."

Jeff groaned. "I hope the next fifteen years aren't filled with bad puns."

"There's no way to know what the future holds..."

Author's Message

I hope you enjoyed reading Truly Unfortunate as much as I did writing it. While this is the end of Truly's story, Knollville curses are only just heating up.

2019 is sure to bring some amazing new stories. I'd love to have you join in the fun.

Until next time...

Happy reading!

ABOUT THE AUTHOR

C.A. King is the recipient of several awards, including: The Hamilton Spectator Readers' Choice Award for 2017 Best Author; The Brant News Readers' Choice Award for 2017 Best Author; Readers' Favourite award in the short story/novella category; the 2017 SIBA Award for Best New Adult; the 2017 SIBA Award for Best Novella; 2018 Readers' Favourite International Book Awards: Gold Medal in the Fiction - Supernatural genre; and 2018 Readers' Favourite International Book Awards: Bronze Medal in the Fiction - New Adult genre

Currently residing in Brantford, Ontario Canada, she lives with her two sons. She began her writing career after the tragic loss of her parents and husband. Redirecting her emotions through writing became therapeutic in her battle with depression and in 2014 she decided to publish some of her works.

Keep in touch with the author online on most social media platforms

Other Titles from C.A. King

The Portal Prophecies

These great titles in C.A. King's The Portal Prophecies series are available now at most online book retailers:

A Keeper's Destiny

A Halloween's Curse

Frost Bitten

Sleeping Sands

Deadly Perceptions

Finding Balance

Volume I (Books 1-3)

Volume II (Books 4-6)

The prophecies are the key to their survival. Can they solve them in time?

Shattering the Effects of Time

Join the Shinning brothers, Jessie, Dezi and Pete as they set out on a quest to save their younger sister. No magic known to them or their friends has ever been able to reverse the grip of time. A few legends, however, exist mentioning ancient items that may hold the key to do exactly that.

This brand new series will take you on a search for the Fountain of Youth and Mermaids; a quest for the Holy Grail; a trip to visit Daryl the mountain guru, in the hunt for the Cinamani Stone; on a search for Ambrosia, the food of the Gods; and other adventures.

Surviving the Sins: Answering the Call

The prophecies are being rewritten. This time someone is using the seven deadly sins: Lust; Gluttony; Greed; Sloth; Wrath; Envy; and Pride, to unlock an ancient evil. The book falls into Jade's hands to answer destiny's call. Can she survive the sins?

Surviving the Sins: Pride

No one is safe when a witch's pride is at stake.

Prudance is back in Pewterclaw, and she isn't about to give up her prestigious status without a fight - especially not because of vampires. As an eighth-generation witch, she plans to do whatever it takes to stop the proposed new legislation from becoming law, including waking the dead for help.

Humility isn't in her vocabulary. With an ego spinning out of control and ancestral power at her fingertips, Prudance weaves a plot to keep Jade and Gavin separated. Will it be enough to satisfy the spirits she summoned?

When her pride costs more than she bargained for, someone has to pay the tab - but who will it be?

Surviving the Sins: Lust

What Mother doesn't know won't hurt her.

Lucinda has spent her entire existence running The Organization and looking after Mother's needs without complaint.

That's about to change. A burning desire had manifested inside her - one she could no longer deny... Lust.

When Constable Safron Black shows up unexpected with news of an imprisoned God, Lucinda unravels. With power fuelling her passion, she'll do anything to make Morynx her mate.

****

Jade and her friends find themselves at a standstill. They have already failed to stop Pride from completing its task and they haven't located any victims for the other six sins. A strange fire in the municipal office puts them hot on the trail of what could be answers. Will they be in time to stop the dial from moving and further opening the way for Morynx?

When Leaves Fall: A Different Point of View Story

Ralph wakes up to what others only experience in a nightmare. Chained to a shed, he has no idea where he is, or who his captor is. His memories a blurred at best. As the days press on he finds himself experiencing a roller coaster of feelings. Hunger, thirst and pain become his only companions. Flashbacks of a happier time are all he has to keep him going. As his situation deteriorates, he finds himself doubting the very things he wants most - a family.

When Leaves Fall is a dramatic-thriller with a twist. Keep the tissue box close for the ending.

Tomoiya's Story

A Vampire Tale. She had a secret but she wasn't the only one who had something to hide.

Book I ~ Escape to Darkness

Book II ~ Collecting Tears

Book III~ Coming Soon

Peach Coloured Daisies: A Cursed by the Gods Story

He couldn't die. An ancient curse meant she always did. This time, that was going to change - one way or another.

When Daisy's grandmother, her last living relative, passes away, she doesn't know where to turn. Things go from bad to worse when a local psychic tells her about a curse. Alone and confused, she ends up in front of her college professor's office, ready to cry her heart out in his arms.

Matt Demi might be the son of a God, but he's living the life of a cursed man. He's had to watch the woman he loves die on her twenty-first birthday countless times. Nothing he does seems to be able to affect the outcome. When she shows up at his office scared out of her wits by a psychic's prediction, he vows this time will be different.

With only three days, Matt will need to embrace a side of him he swore off long ago to save her, but will he lose himself in the process?

Flower Shields: A Four Horsemen Novel

Meet the four horsemen: Michael, Gabrielle, Uriel and Raphael. For centuries their job has been to guard the gates of hell, making sure they never open. Without the keys, there was never any real threat. That's about to change. There are rumours on the horizon that demon followers unearthed scrolls that explain exactly how to find the lost keys. This new battle is a race to see which side locates them first.

Michael couldn't care less about the love story behind how and why the world was created. In fact, nothing matters to him other than keeping the gates to hell closed. If one of the lost keys ever fell into the wrong hands, all humanity would be doomed. He's not going to let that happen - at any cost.

****

Tara's life is nothing short of a disaster. She's managed to flunk out of college with about the same amount of dignity as every relationship she's been in. The only constant in her life has been her love for flowers. When she's attacked at work, a stranger comes to her aid. Michael might be good-looking, but he's also arrogant, bossy and crazy. He's also her only chance to figure out who attacked her and why. Should she follow her heart and trust him - or listen to her head and run?

Drawing Strength From Words: A Four Horsemen Novel

Meet the four horsemen: Michael, Gabrielle, Uriel and Raphael.

For centuries their sole purpose has been guarding the sealed gates to hell. Without keys, there was never any real threat. That was about to change...

For Gabrielle, protecting mankind was merely a job for which she received little credit. The vast insecurities of men altered history itself, portraying her as a masculine brute. Taking a back seat to her brothers seemed the right thing to do, but left a bitter taste in her mouth and an impenetrable barricade shielding her heart.

****

Ryder bounced around the system from the moment both his parents were killed. Between that and run-ins with the law for crimes he never committed, it seemed the whole world was conspiring against him. Never growing attached to anyone was rule number one: a rule he'd never broken until a white-haired vixen, with blocks of ice on her shoulders, walked right into his life. Melting through those frosty layers became all that mattered, even if that meant sacrificing himself in the process.

Miracles Not Included

A heartfelt romantic story about: life; love; loss; and learning to love again. If only life came with instructions and a warning label ~ Miracles Not Included.

****

Chris was born to be a writer. Even the smallest of details couldn't pass without notice, often becoming part of a plot for her next novel. The one thing she never saw coming was her husband's sudden illness.

Jason loved his wife from the moment they met. Nothing could ever change that - nothing except the death sentence he'd been handed - a terminal cancer diagnosis.

His story was ending: Hers was starting a new chapter and more than one miracle was needed to turn the page.

Twisted Tales of a Dead End Street

A paranormal mystery laced with comedic undertones: Twisted Tales of a Dead End Street.

Nine neighbours were invited to the mysterious dinner party at 9 Nine Street. Their host, the owner of the mansion, had more planned for the evening than just roast beef.

When the secret of their quiet street was revealed, everything changed, blurring the lines between the tangible and the paranormal.

Was the number nine the difference between life and death? Would any of them survive long enough to uncover the truth? They would each soon find out this wasn't a simple case of who-done-it so much as one of what was being done and by whom.

Shot Through The Heart: A Faerie Tale

A tale of two worlds - one filled with magic; the other void of it. But what happened to those trapped between the two? Adelia was about to find out...

Magic and structure were the foundations of her existence. Temptation controlled the ability to destroy everything she knew. The world of men held a powerful allure over her heart, waking that which had long been dormant. It enticed her, snagging her in a web of emotions.

A decision had to be made. Was feeling love for the first time worth sacrificing magic and immortality?

Do Not Open Until Halloween

When eighteen year old Caitlin agreed to babysit her eccentric Aunt's two cats and house, she had no idea that Justin was finally going to ask her for a date the same weekend. Torn between family and crush, she chose to take her best friends' suggestion to heart, arranging a small Friday night gathering. Little did she know a fairy was about to crash the party with trouble hot on her wings.

Caitlin will have to dig deep to find even a smidgen of belief in magic or there won't be any hope of saving her new friend from being hunted.

In this young adult fantasy, award-winning author, C.A. King, explores the answer to one of the questions readers have always wanted to ask...

Where do fairies come from?